ONE-WAY ———————————

DIDIER VAN CAUWELAERT | # ONE-WAY

translated by **MARK POLIZZOTTI**

OTHER

Other Press • New York

Ouvrage publié avec le concours du Ministère français chargé de la culture–Centre National du Livre.

We wish to express our appreciation to the French Ministry of Culture–CNL–for its assistance in the preparation of the translation.

Production Editor: Robert D. Hack

This book was set in 11 pt Electra LH Regular by Alpha Graphics of Pittsfield, NH.

10 9 8 7 6 5 4 3 2 1

Library of Congress Cataloging-in-Publication Data

Cauwelaert, Didier van, 1960–
    [Aller simple. English]
    One-way : a novel / by Didier van Cauwelaert ; translated from the French by Mark Polizzotti.
      p. cm.
    ISBN 1-59051-086-0 (hardcover : alk. paper)
    I. Polizzotti, Mark. II. Title.
    PQ2663.A8473 A4413 2003
    843'.914—dc21

2003010266

ONE-WAY

1

I started out in life as an accidental foundling. A child stolen by mistake along with the car. We were parked on the crosswalk and, for years afterward, when I didn't clear my plate, Mamita would say that the tow truck was going to come and get me. So then I ate too fast and finished by puking it all up, but in a way it was better: it kept me from gaining weight. I was the adopted one and I knew my place.

With gypsies, children are sacred. They have to be as fat as possible, for prestige. They're considered kings from ages zero to four—after that, they're on their own. I made it on my own without ever being a king, so I didn't have so far to fall. I hugged the walls, said nothing. I was the thinnest. If you do your best to be forgotten, eventually you succeed.

Often, at night, the tow truck came to take away my illegally parked car and haul it to the junkyard, leaving me to be crushed inside sheet metal. Luckily, in Mamita's trailer, one of the kings was always bawling his lungs out; that interrupted the dream while I was still alive, and I could get back to sleep. I knew I was safe and warm among those king babies covered in chains and medallions that clanked in the dark. I appreciated it all the more in that my fate—as they never got tired of telling me—had hung on a single vote, in the elders' council. Old Vasile, the Rom who had stolen me without realizing I was asleep in my basket on the back seat, amid all the Christmas presents— he'd put everything he had into the argument, against the Manouches who wanted to send me back. Since there were no registration papers in the glove compartment, he considered me a sign from above. Nobody argued with him because he was already very old at the time, and according to our customs senility is wisdom.

The car was an Ami 6 of the Citroën family, so they named me Ami 6 in its honor. Those were my roots, after all. Over time, it slurred into Aziz. Mamita, who was born in Romania, where she was sterilized by the Nazis, always said it was a bad idea to Arabize me like that, because when I was small I looked French—as she saw it, the names you're given rub off on you. Personally, I don't care. I'm perfectly happy being an Arab because there are a lot of us and people leave us alone. When I started dealing in car radios and I needed fake papers in case of arrest, I also got a family name: Kemal. I don't know where they came up with that one—maybe K's were just in that year.

Sometimes I thought about my original parents, who must have filed a report and waited for the ransom demand and still kept hoping, so long as my body hadn't been found. One day, I told myself, I'd put an ad in the *Provençal*: "Child stolen around Christmas in a Citroën Ami 6 seeks his parents. Reply Aziz Kemal, blue minivan opposite the Volkswagen marked 'Vasile's Pizza,' Floral Valley housing development, North Marseilles." But I always put it off. When you've gotten yourself more or less accepted into a family, you're not so eager to try your luck a second time. I preferred to maintain the doubt and nurture my dream. Since I didn't know where I came from, I was content to be here.

I often imagined I was the son of a forward on the Olympiques de Marseille soccer team, whose mechanic had lent him an Ami 6 while the Mercedes was in for repairs. Another time, I was heir to the Savons de Marseille soap fortune. Or the last in a family of dock workers, with one unemployment check for twelve. On rainy days, I told myself they'd just had another kid to replace me.

And then, when I was eighteen, they let me in on the truth. A different truth, whether harder or simpler I don't know. Old Vasile hadn't stolen my Ami 6. He had crashed into it with the pizza oven Volkswagen as it was trying to make an illegal pass at the Frioune bend. Parents killed instantly. He had pulled me from the wreckage before it burst into flames, and there you have it: I knew the rest. Vasile had never gotten over it; he had never again touched a steering wheel or lit his oven, which was why I had always known his combo Volkswagen to be on blocks, covered in ivy, with a Blessed Virgin in his pizza oven.

At first I was kind of touched that the whole development had led me on for so long, just to spare my feelings—and also a little annoyed, to tell the truth. I put on my best T-shirt and went with dignity to thank Vasile for having saved my life and not just sped off. He drew a wrinkled finger from beneath his plaid blanket and uttered in a cavernous voice, his eyes staring into the void, "Begotten not made, of one being with the Father, through whom all things were made."

That must have been a riddle, and I didn't know the answer. But by now he was completely dotty and we only took him out on special occasions, so maybe there was no answer.

I felt sad for my parents, of course. Even if it's hard to cry for someone without knowing them. And then I consoled myself with the thought that at least they hadn't suffered from my absence. The funny thing is, in the months that followed, what I especially missed was the little want ad I wrote to them in my head before falling asleep, polishing it, improving it, wording it better. The little ad that

I always kept in my heart to dictate one day, just in case. Now it no longer had anything to do with anyone. I was the orphan of a sentence.

But anyway, life went on. I found myself in Marseilles, then, as a provisional Moroccan, with a residence card that required a fee with each renewal. It seemed to me that, rather than making me false papers, they could just as easily have given me French nationality, but it's also true that I hadn't wanted to pay the higher price. I have my principles. The money I earn from my car radios I give straight to the development: it goes toward reimbursing my childhood expenses, not toward fattening up the neighborhood forgers. In any case, if you ask me, race isn't something you buy. It's like your eye color or the weather outside, things that just happen to you without asking your opinion. And besides, if people need fake papers to realize I'm French, then I'd rather stay an Arab. I've got my pride.

No, the only place that troubles me is the soccer field. That's where I really feel divided. Playing for the Floral Valley Roms against the Rocher-Mirabeau Beurs[1] made me feel like a traitor. And not only a traitor but a usurper: I know full well that the gypsies don't consider me one of their own. A *gadjo* center-forward, even when he scores a goal against his own race, might be a good center-forward

---

[1] Slang term for Arab immigrants (*trans.*).

but he's still a *gadjo*, an outsider. That's why I finally became a ref.

In the scrapes between developments, things are easier: instinctively, I've always sided with my adoptive family, even though it bothers me to beat the crap out of the Rocher-Mirabeau gang. It's hard not to recognize a blood brother when he's bleeding. So I avoid fighting as much as I can, and they take me for a coward, but that's not important so long as the girl I'm in love with isn't ashamed of me in front of the others—and, as it happens, no one knows about us.

Lila is nineteen, like me. We've known each other since we were kids and now we have to be careful, because of my origins. Her brothers have chosen her a Manouche like them, a purebred Sainte-Marie: Rajko, the Mercedes specialist. So when Lila and I run into each other in the development, it's just hello-goodbye and eyes turned away. But once a week she takes the train, I swipe a scooter, and we meet up in the Niolon inlet, which is the loveliest spot in the world—at the time, I'd never left the Bouches-du-Rhône.

Like her mother, Lila sees people's lives in their palms. All she's said about me is that mine'll end soon but that I'll start over again at a crossroads. She has black hair, eyes that burn, the smell of lindens in June, and red or blue skirts down to her ankles that fly up when she dances—but I'll stop there because, given what happened later, it hurts too much to remember.

Hundreds of times she told me about India, the land she came from and never knew; about its ceremonies, the sacred cows, the flowered pyre where they tossed the widow when the dead man was a purebred—I wasn't really listening. I don't listen very much in life, except at school, and I don't go there anymore. But from the first day we made love, she fully clothed and me from behind to re-spect ourselves before the marriage—*her* marriage—all of that ceased to exist. We were free and alone in the world and I finally felt at home. She told me "I love you" in her language; I don't have any language other than the one I speak every day—no language to myself, I mean, secret— so I didn't say anything, but my heart was in it. I thought that after her marriage we wouldn't have to respect our-selves anymore, and we could love each other face to face.

In the evening, at the confabs, everyone recalls his ori-gins, his traditions, the country where he packed up his roots; laments the stainless steel that destroyed the glory of the Kalderash, tinker-coppersmiths from generation to generation; lists between two strums of the guitar and three harmonica solos the persecutions, pogroms, and town or-dinances that landed him, wanderer in his mind and trailer on blocks, at Floral Valley in the Bouches-du-Rhône. Me, I sit there and say nothing. I nod out of respect, but my mind is elsewhere. I don't like hearing about where oth-ers came from. I'm perfectly happy to have no history, apart from the Ami 6, but it hurts to be the only one.

Happiness was when I used to go to school. Happiness was learning. I invented another family for myself alone, with words and figures that I could rearrange as I pleased, add, conjugate, subtract, and everyone understood me. At the blackboard, when I recited battles and names of rivers, they listened as if I were telling my own story. Millions of corpses, floods, and instances of man's hatred were transformed into good grades. The best reward, for me, was learning the contours and climate of other countries, not only because people came from there, but simply because they existed. And that was only the beginning: there were so many things left to learn, I'd be busy for a lifetime.

But I had to leave school in the middle of sixth grade, because Floral Valley doesn't believe in useless mouths. At first you're a *chouf*, a lookout on foot; at seven you nab your first handbags; at eleven you become a "lark," a lookout on wheels, and you quit school. That's how it is.

My geography teacher, Mr. Giraudy, said he was sorry to see me go. We hadn't really talked much outside of class, because talking bothers me. I never manage to capture the right words. Like fish that struggle when you hook them— it's so much nicer just to watch them swim. Mr. Giraudy said that life wasn't perfect, and he should know: he was fifty. According to him, in other parts of Marseilles there were normal schools, without graffiti or drugs or rapes or brawls, and I deserved better because I actually wanted to learn. He looked so sad, I had never seen anyone so sad, and I thought to myself that maybe it was better for me to quit school if it made you that sad.

He wished me luck and gave me this amazing book, an atlas weighing six pounds called *Legends of the World*. I kept my mouth shut so I wouldn't cry, because they had always told me an Arab is proud. Instead I thought, "May the Prophet always walk with you." It wasn't true religion, just something I'd heard, but I meant it.

The day I stole my first car radio, a Grundig, I mailed it to him as a thank-you gift, with a note: "From Aziz, class 6B, for your kindness." I promised myself that later, when I was old enough to drive, I'd steal him the car to go with it, because we'd always seen Mr. Giraudy taking the bus. But little by little I forgot about it, and then it was too late, because of what happened.

Around the fire, at the evening confab, while the others told of Romania and Turkey and northern India, all the places they'd been driven from, I memorized the legends of the world, especially Arabia. Since no one was sure which country I came from, it felt more real to learn the dreams of a place than its everyday reality, the kind you found in the pages of the *Provençal*, which I used for wrapping my car radios before I sold them.

And out of the corner of my eye, between the flames consuming the crates, I watched Lila, who avoided my gaze, sitting next to Rajko, her intended, the Mercedes specialist, who accompanied the recital of persecutions on his guitar. Me, I accompanied my pain by reciting to myself the story of the lovers from Imilchil, about an Ait Brahim who fell madly in love with an Ait Yazza, the enemy tribe. From their tears were born Lake Isli, the Lake of the Betrothed, and Lake Tislit, the Lake of the Beloved, in which the families drowned the lovers separately to prevent the misalliance on page 143 of my atlas.

One July afternoon, on the rocks of the inlet after lovemaking, I gently evoked Ait Brahim in Lila's ear. She thought I was talking about a pal in the Beur development and dove into the water to hunt for sea urchins.

When I venture into the French part of Marseilles, to go inspect the new car radios and get an idea of their market value, I see the families of other young people and sometimes I wish I were in their shoes. But it passes. The tenderness I sometimes miss in Floral Valley is replaced by brotherhood in action. In that regard, I'm a full member of the clan: I have a winning smile, agile hands, and I run fast.

One of our specialties is the Italian Attack—which the Italians call the Gypsy Attack, but they're in the minority. You pass by on a scooter, you slit their tire at a red light, you stop to help them change it, and you make off with their car. The police, moreover, have advised people who can't avoid driving through our neighborhood not to stop at red lights. That's all well and good, but if they don't stop we just crash into them. They come out with their no-fault report and we hold them up: it's a variant, the Belgian Attack. We bring the car back to the development and strip it in teams: the engine parts team, the tire group, the headlights and accessories crew, and the radio team—me. We work mainly with Mercedes and, so as not to complicate our lives with inventory, a guy like Rajko, for instance, works only on special order. You tell him, "Rajko, I need a cylinder head gasket for a 500 SL," and you have it the next day.

When only the carcass remains, we drag it out to the avenue at the edge of the city for the public works to cart away, otherwise the wrecks would just pile up. Our place isn't a dump. Floral Valley is our pride and joy. We even planted flowers to go with the name—which shows that Mamita was right: over time, the name becomes the thing.

In the same way, as Aziz Kemal, I went through my Muslim phase when I was about fifteen. But it didn't last long: I loved Lila's mouth too much to cover it with a veil. I gave Saïd back his Koran—he's the watchman at the Ducs development, a champion who has so far managed to keep the pushers out of his buildings with nothing but a baseball bat—and I continued to root for the Olympiques de Marseille.

Life is calm in Floral Valley, and police raids are few and far between. I should say that any cop who tried to check IDs in the northern quarter would first be immediately escorted to the border, and then the superintendent would chew him out, because the measure the superintendent adopted to fight crime here is to decide we don't exist. Officially, North Marseilles is a desert. Our developments are no longer marked on the map. Some thirty titular police remain for two hundred thousand nonexistent residents, and because of that it's gotten to the point where we protect them, like an endangered species.

Not to boast, but I think the superintendent is pretty clever, in his way: if we beat up a cop, we know perfectly well that any charges he brings will never make it to court because of the statistics, so we feel sorry for him and, rather than break his head, we opt for self-discipline. Since the local patrol comes around in two teams of five cars, one from noon to 7 PM and the other from 7 to 4 in the morning, we make sure to work between 4 and noon, when they're asleep, and everybody's happy. To thank us for our tact, they even built us our own market where we go help ourselves for free with our carts. It saves us having to break into Leclerc and Casino, which are reserved for the local old folks who have no other choice but to pay at the register. We respect those old folks. Especially since in most cases they've owned their apartments for decades, which now, with us nearby, have lost three-quarters of their value.

No, overall, North Marseilles works pretty well. We even get entertainment from Paris from time to time. Committees that propose solutions for improving our quality of life. Last year it was sunlight. They really did improve our lot: they razed the old high-rises in the next development over, as if delinquency stemmed from too many floors. In that regard, there's no danger: gypsies, even adopted ones like me, can't stand verticals. We couldn't live in a high-rise. Or in a low-rise, for that matter—it's like a high-rise, but on its side, and that must not be very good for delinquency either. As soon as a unit becomes vacant in a low-rise, the housing office boards it up instead of renting it out again: I think it must be cheaper than putting the place back in usable shape.

The day the committee came to Floral Valley went well enough. We were very nice and offered them a pernod to calm their nerves, frazzled because they'd just come from visiting the Comorians in Basse-Robière where they'd gotten a fridge dropped on their heads. A little music, Manouche jazz, flamenco, Gypsy Kings, and you relax. The committee thanked us for our welcome. They took away with them the baskets that the children showed them, thinking they were presents. Afterward, they stated on the news that the "Bohemians" were not comfortable in their trailers, and that this was the source of all their problems—easy to say if you don't know. In place of the dilapidated shack we used as a mechanic's shop, they built us low-cost Bouygues houses.

We were pleased as punch. We let them build, without stealing the cement from the site, since it was for us and we were eager to have them finish. After the final touches were put on, they came back with the superintendent, a TV crew, and a man from Bouygues to officially hand us the keys: the locks were already gone. So were the doors, for that matter, and the windows, and the sinks, and the johns. We'd stripped the whole thing and sold it off piece by piece. All that was left were the shingles, which we were saving for winter: we'd get a better price for them then. The man from Bouygues pulled a face like an unearthed corpse, and he told the TV people to get lost, and the superintendent didn't know what to do with himself. But we were perfectly content with the houses even so, don't go thinking otherwise: they provided a nice view from the trailer windows. They gave the place atmosphere, we said to flatter them. We repeated our congratulations and if you'll come this way, the buffet is served.

They didn't have any of the celebratory lunch we'd prepared for them, with foods they were familiar with, swiped specially from the Fauchon outlet in Marignane. We were left speechless after their departure, with our tons of jellied eggs and salmon quiches. We ate them all the same, but we were disappointed.

Pignol came by to have us sign the complaint, since we were our own victims. He helped us polish off the buffet.

Pignol is my childhood buddy. We used to know each other in school, but he stayed there longer than I did and sometimes he wishes he hadn't, when he sees the life I lead. Back then he wanted to work in trains, but he couldn't pass the exam so he followed in his old man's footsteps. It's at moments like this that you thank your lucky stars for being an orphan. Especially since they stuck the police academy between two hot spots, so the trainees wouldn't feel cut off from the population. In that regard, it was a success: they took their classes behind metal fences, besieged, bombarded with rocks and beer cans to teach them their trade. They aren't allowed out of the bunker alone, and a paddy wagon brings them back to their dorm at night—it's what they call "being on the right side of the law." Their dorm is located in Jean-Jaurès, another pretty tough development where they're guarded all night long by patrol cars, whose only job is to protect the apprentice cops from their future victims. The lesson they take away from it, of course, is hatred, and since there's no outlet for it here, it creates useless vocations and gets them shipped off to developments in Lyon, where things are less civilized.

On Sundays, I'd go visit Pignol in his visiting room, and I was a bit sad for him. So good in French, and here he was regressing between courses in marksmanship and games of pinochle. His future, past the bars of his school, promised him nothing in return for his wasted youth, and his father, one of the instructors, treated him like a little kid, a wimp, and a sissy. That's how it is: a lot of old cops, who used to make the law in Marseilles back when, now have only their young recruits to take it out on.

I tried to help Pignol the best I could. When he was doing his night patrol training, I told him the danger zones to avoid; I even tipped him off to two or three little red-handed jobs so he'd get his diploma. It's normal to return favors: back in school, when we had dictations, he was the one I'd copy off.

One evening when he was crying in his beer, I told him a legend from my atlas. This one took place in Cuba. It was the story of Jose Luis, a boy our age who every night turned into a jaguar, thanks to voodoo magic that teaches you how to come out of your dreams as anything you want. And Jose Luis spent his nights trying to woo a female jaguar who wanted no part of him. He was very unhappy and, instead of doing his jaguar job, hunting to feed his cubs, he sank into despair. And it was the same during the day, when he would neglect cutting his sugarcane to sigh over someone else's wife — to the point where the voodoo spirits got fed up, and one morning they found Jose Luis on his bed in his human skin, devoured by the jaguar of his dreams.

Pignol had shrugged his shoulders and said I was a utopian. I was disappointed that he didn't understand the meaning of the story, which seemed clear to me: if you indulge in despair, you end up consumed by the dreams you never got over.

Still, I looked up *utopian* in the dictionaries at the bookstore. It was a Mr. Morus who came up with the term in 1516, from the Greek words meaning "that which does not exist anywhere." I liked that.

From that day on, until the adventure that happened to me, I didn't tell any legends to anybody. I kept them for myself. It was my personal reality, which concerned neither Lila nor Pignol. And gradually, I believe, the old red-and-gold book, all dog-eared and worn from so much reading, became my real homeland, my country of origin. There was a story where I often went, the one from Austria. A swimmer was bathing in a pond and went closer to admire the water lilies. He found them so beautiful and peaceful; it made a change from the villagers who threw rocks at him because he was a Jew. So he put out his hand to caress one of the water lilies and, under his touch, the stalk that had wrapped around his leg retracted and pulled him to the bottom of the pond. There he discovered a marvelous world with mermaids and talking seaweed, where he could breathe more easily than up above.

At night, I wished I could caress the water lilies—and not only because of the villagers. Raised among sedentary nomads, I often had such a strong desire to leave, but leaving by yourself is a bit like staying. Lila wouldn't follow me unless she was a widow, and Rajko was in excellent health.

From legend to legend, in my minivan with no wheels mounted on blocks, I sometimes lost my footing, imagined the bottom of the pond that surely awaited me. Someday, the words I caressed would drag me down below the surface, and there would be no one left above the open book.

2

We had just been swimming among the boats in the small port squeezed into a hollow in the cliffs, which the old station overlooks with its blue shutters, half-erased frieze, and sloping roof raked by swallows. We had made love in the water, in the shadow of the UCPA climbing rock[2] that cream-white students dove from, amid cries and gasps that covered ours, and we were quietly sipping a *perroquet* on the terrace of Chez Francis, admiring the inlet in the afternoon light, when Lila gathered her long, thick hair in a braid, began to wring it out, and said:

"Here's the deal."

---

[2] The UCPA (Union des Centres Plein Air) is a national organization that promotes outdoor sports, notably rock climbing (*trans.*).

In a tone that took me by surprise. As if she were stating an unalterable fact, which at first I thought had to do with the weather: heavy clouds were gathering above the viaduct, and droplets of water had begun splashing on our arms. I said it would be better next week. She said no, in a still darker voice, and then I understood. At the last Saintes-Maries festival, she had made the pilgrimage with Rajko and it was now just a matter of time before they put together a dowry: her brothers were about to make a big score, selling the thousand reinforced shutters they'd stolen in December back to the housing office. On the one hand, it made my heart ache, but on the other, I had a lot of respect for Rajko. He was a great mechanic: he'd shown me how to resolve even the toughest anti-theft problems with car radios, including welded face plates and secret access codes. Lila could do much worse, as fiancés go. I knew she had opened the royal gates to him, but I wasn't jealous. All I asked was to keep coming in the back way. After all, "love does not consist in gazing at each other but in looking together in the same direction," as Mr. de Saint-Exupéry once said, in a dictation where I had made only three mistakes.

"So that's it," I said. "Your brothers have sold the doors."

She shrugged her beautiful naked shoulders, which I had perhaps held above the water for the last time, and said, "We knew it was coming."

"But we can keep seeing each other," I said in a strained voice, with a rock in my throat.

"No. Rajko found out about us. He's agreed to marry me anyway, but I had to swear it was over between you and me, that you no longer exist."

I said all right. And I gave her a lift back to the station. Our affair ended on a platform full of sunlight, wet bathing suits, salty skin, and happy couples. Watching her climb into the rail car, her skirt glued to her ass, it did no good to imagine her ten years down the road, with her mother's 250 pounds—heredity didn't make me feel any better. We could have gotten fat together, but there you had it: I'd stay skinny. Still, a strange glimmer of hope kept me from being too miserable. I've always had these little premonitions. I can't read palms like Lila, who kept telling me I had a double life in my lines—faithful as I was, that bothered me a bit—but when I can't manage to suffer, it's usually a sign.

When Rajko was gunned down by a guard ten days before their wedding, during his midnight shopping spree at the Mercedes showroom, I thanked the Saint Marys, the Good Mother, Allah, and the Olympiques—all the gods of Marseilles. This wasn't mean-spiritedness, it was love: I had simply prayed for Lila to be a widow someday soon, before she gained too much weight.

Everyone in Floral Valley knew that Rajko had asked for an advance on the marriage, so she was damaged goods— and that was my chance. I went to see Mateo, her older brother, and offered to take her off his hands. As a dowry, I promised to supply a dozen Pioneer DVD players and forty Bose speakers. They would never do better, for second-hand. A vote was taken in the elders' caravan and I won by two—both belonging to old Vasile, who no longer knows his own name but gets to vote twice because of his age. Mateo had to bow to their decision, with rage in his heart. Manouches can be funny sometimes: they'd rather see a girl dishonored for life, alone, than palmed off on a *gadjo* who would erase the stain by taking her far away.

Lila did not jump for joy when she heard about my victory. She told me, with a sad sigh, "Don't get your hopes up, Aziz."

But I thought it was for appearances' sake, since she was still in mourning. I only understood her reaction a month later, during our engagement banquet, when my first life ended.

I had chosen Café Marchelli, at the outskirts of our development, on an overpass above the off-ramp. That's where drug deals are made, because we don't want any of that at home. Matter of principle. *We're* in business, and that's what keeps the sector going: stealing cars creates a market for new ones, whereas smack just kills the customer—not to mention the expense of the first few free shots, to create a taste for dependency. Personally, I spit on pushers. And when I find death threats on my minivan, I just paint them over.

But anyway, it was there, at Café Marchelli, that I'd decided to hold my engagement banquet with Lila, because they have real tablecloths and a gourmet menu and banquet decorations—and besides, over there, at the outer limits of our territory, it was already like being on honeymoon.

I had invited all 250 pounds of her mother, whom it took four people to carry in the wicker throne, as well as her twelve brothers with their wives and their uncles, and they started talking in their language, Sinto, which I don't understand a word of—at Mamita's, may her soul rest in peace, the dialect was Kalderash. In any case, between different clans, we can only understand each other in French. The atmosphere was a bit tense, and it was a shame because I'd done everything right—at least as far as the decorations were concerned. For the rest, I never got to see for myself, because of the police raid.

Since Pignol was on vacation, no one had warned me. The four of them walked in, guns drawn, hands up and face the wall. We, out of reflex, with our glasses raised to make a toast, moved as if to invite them for a drink; they took it all wrong and we were slammed against the walls, frisked, shoved, treated like gypsies—I won't say "like Arabs," because actually I was the only one. I asked what it was we'd done and they answered, "Shut your face." I figured they were just showing off for Pignol's replacement, a girl. They'd come to make an example, and since they had only one seat left in the car, they took me. They probably thought it would limit the ethnic conflict, and they weren't mistaken.

The Manouches really didn't lift a finger to help me. Mateo even slapped Lila, who was screaming "Aziz!" The owner, Marchelli, looking like he'd seen it all before and all in a day's work, counted the spots on the glass he was wiping. I heard him call out "Goodbye, gentlemen" as they hauled me out to the tinkling of the bell above the door. Since I'd paid in advance, I imagine they went ahead and devoured my engagement banquet.

Lila chased the police car for a while; she ran two hundred yards with her white shoes in her hand and cursing — she was really something, vocabulary straight from the gutter and a hell of a lung capacity — and then she stopped, shrugged, and gave us the finger, but I didn't understand what she meant by it. Through the rear window, I saw her turn back to Café Marchelli, where they must have been attacking the main courses, and it was strange, but I knew things were finished between us, just like that: instinct. Between a fiancé stolen from you and a meal growing cold, she had made her choice. Maybe I was being unfair: she *had* run after me. But in my way, I was like Astirios of Macedonia, the Greek fortune teller from page 115, who had read in a chicken liver that his master, Epirandas, was going to kill him, and told him so. I always know before anyone else the harm they'll choose to do to me.

They threw me into the cage where they put the people they round up before sorting them out. I was a bit embarrassed to look so elegant amid all the others — white Daniel Hechter suit with fashionably cuffed trousers and an Oxford shirt with stripes to match my pure silk Pierre Cardin tie—but I didn't have a chance to explain that it was my engagement day; they took me out again almost immediately for the confrontation. And there I got a shock.

In the commissioner's office, sitting in a chair, hands folded over his pot belly, I found Place Vendôme, the jeweler from the Panier who'd sold me Lila's ring, because an engagement present is not something you steal, if you're honorable. I wanted a prestigious firm with the name on the box, *Place Vendôme de Paris*, white on red leather; it was superb. The commissioner ordered me to "sit the fuck down! sorry—sit down": the superintendent must have told him no slip-ups. I sat down, and stayed there gaping as I listened to Place Vendôme declare that I'd burgled him. The commissioner asked me if I recognized the jewel box. Of course I recognized it: they'd found it in my pocket when they searched me at the café, because I wasn't exactly going to give my gift while we were still on the aperitifs—what did they take me for? But I'd paid him for his ring, eight thousand two hundred francs, if you don't mind! Place Vendôme said the price was right, but I'd still stolen it.

The commissioner asked if I had a receipt. I shrugged: I wasn't going to give the ring wrapped in a receipt, I've got manners. He answered that anything I said would be used against me, and that gave me a laugh, because really, let's be honest. And then I felt like crying because I remembered that I'd forgotten to ask for a receipt: I wasn't in the habit of buying things.

"Ask Place Vendôme," I said. "He's got the receipt."
And I felt that whether I said that or said nothing, it was
all the same. Place Vendôme de Paris sighed while shaking his head, eyes rolled to the ceiling. I tried to sock him
one but the others shoved me back into the chair, tearing
a sleeve of the Daniel Hechter, and I no longer said anything except to ask when Pignol was coming back from
vacation, and that wasn't very smart either. They threw me
back in the hole, yelling at me as if I'd tried to smear their
colleague, and I cried like a little girl among the junkies
scattered around the cell, because this was the first time
I'd suffered injustice.

The I thought of my atlas, which I'd left at home, in
my minivan that didn't lock, and if someone stole it from
me it would be worse than losing Lila—I liked her enough,
because we'd grown up together, but *Legends of the World*
was a gift from a man who wasn't obliged, who had shown
me the joy of learning, which was more sacred than anything on earth. Those were my roots and they were going
to take everything from me and they hadn't even removed
my tie to keep me from hanging myself. I was no longer
worth anything, and I felt like a coward because I still
wanted to live.

The day passed as if it were already a memory, a memory
of nothing. They had forgotten me. It was the end of everything and of nothing much when you got down to it, but I
had no complaints: I'd had nineteen years of happiness
without causing anyone harm, except for Place Vendôme

whose neck I'd wrung, or at least the fork's in place of his. Afterward I ate their porridge with my fingers and it was really something, it was my engagement banquet, and besides I didn't give a shit. Lila could end up a whore at a nickel a pound and too bad for her, I had loved her so much for so long, I had never loved anyone but her, life was so beautiful with her in the ocean at Niolon, and Vasile should have let me roast in my Ami 6 at the Frioune bend.

Night fell, and all around me people were snoring. I lay there with eyes wide open, telling myself everything and nothing, just to fill my head; otherwise I would have thought of my atlas and that would have been too sad.

The next day they put me in a single cell. Some guy I didn't know in a dark suit came to look at me, asked me to stand up, turn around, and smile. Then he looked relieved and said to the commissioner, "Well, there you go, this one will do just fine."

The commissioner thanked me and they shut the cell door again. To pass the time, I thought about Mamadou M'Ba in the Ethiopian legend; I tried to convince myself that they were going to sell me as a slave in the market-place, but it didn't get very far. The only image I could keep in my head was Rajko's. His smile, his guitar, his handshake and magic fingers. He had taught me my trade; he would surely have made Lila happy and he had died for nothing. I asked his forgiveness.

And then Pignol returned from his vacation. I thought he was going to turn me loose, but I could see right away, from his face. He said well, here's how it is, it was nothing against me, and I had to understand. I said I was trying to understand, but Place Vendôme's shitty trick was stuck in my craw. He said Place Vendôme was just a detail. I said oh really. But it was true: the important thing was my atlas. I told him to go to my place, and he answered that it was already done: his colleagues had gone to make a search, but they hadn't found anything.

"Nothing?" I asked.

He put a hand on my shoulder. My house had already been visited, and when he said "visited". . . . The minivan was all that remained. The carcass. I didn't insist. Asking about the atlas would have meant being hurt for nothing. With us it's like with animals, and that's normal: we help each other when we're there, and when someone's wounded we finish him off, in the interests of the community. That's just the way it is.

Pignol added that for my papers, really, I could have done better. Such obvious forgeries were almost an insult. I didn't say anything, because it was Place Vendôme who had supplied them and that too would turn against me, since I didn't have a receipt. The jeweler did favors in both directions, that much was known: half snitch, half fence. He had the prefecture's seal of approval and I didn't measure up.

"They're going to send you home, Aziz."

I said thanks, but it wasn't worth it. I no longer had a "home" and I'd lost Lila; might as well let justice take its course.

"You don't understand, Aziz. Sending you home means back to your country."

"My country?"

"Morocco."

It took me a while to understand, and then I remembered that my papers said I was Moroccan, but they could just as easily have put down Tunisian, Algerian, or Syrian. It was just to make it look real, it wasn't a proof of anything.

"They want to set an example, Aziz. They're forced to send you back where you come from."

So then I said, "Listen, I'm happy to be an example, but I've lived my whole life as a foreigner in France. I'm not going to start over again as a foreigner in a country where I'll be the only one to know I don't actually come from there. I already had enough trouble with the gypsies. I'm just Aziz, the son of Ami 6 by Citroën, and I'm from Marseilles, just like you, Pignol, for Christ's sake! You can see it. You can hear it!"

But I knew damn well I wasn't convincing anybody: even my own face had turned against me. I was betrayed through and through. To keep from crying in front of him, I asked him to thank the superintendent for me.

"It comes from higher than that, Aziz. The government has passed measures against illegal aliens. I mean, *for* illegal aliens. It's a joint operation between Human Rights and the Immigration Office."

And he explained that, basically, to fight racism in France, they had to send the immigrants back home. I kept my mouth shut, but it seemed like a strange idea to fight an idea by putting it into practice. He added that I'd be taking the plane tomorrow morning at Marignane, and that a civil servant specially assigned to me, a "humanitarian attaché" they called him, would accompany me to Morocco to make sure everything went well, settle me back in, find me work, a place to live, and, as the ministry memo said, "send France welcome news of its friends who have returned home."

He finished by saying that the humanitarian attaché should have been there that morning, but he'd missed the express train and had to wait for the next one. I said things were off to a good start, but it was to play it cool, be the kind of guy who takes life with a grain of salt. In reality, I was completely crushed; Pignol too. A colleague called to him; he made a gesture of impotence, then he shut me back in my hole and went to have lunch. They brought me my pail, with the fork I'd twisted instead of Place Vendôme, and again I ate with my fingers, and it was the same food, and time stood still, except that tomorrow I was going to take the plane, and I waited.

At twenty to five, Pignol returned. He avoided my gaze, but I'd had time to think and I felt more reassured. He announced in a bland voice, "Your attaché has arrived."

I asked, legs crossed, casual as anything, "Did they give him my papers?"

"Yes."

"Good, well, there you have it, then: he saw they were fakes."

"No."

I stopped looking at my nails.

"All he saw was that your residence card has expired."

He sat down next to me on the mattress, hands between his knees and head bowed. My worry returned all at once.

"But didn't you tell him they're fakes?"

He didn't answer immediately. He took his chewing gum from his mouth and began rolling it between his thumb and index finger. When the ball was completely smooth, he stated that, in any case, like it or not, I was in an irregular situation.

I protested, "But, Pignol, that's what I've been in since I was born!"

He screwed up his face to make me stop talking.

"There's something you have to understand, Aziz. For three days the Brigade has had these guys on its ass, they keep demanding illegal aliens, illegal aliens, illegal aliens! They're in a real state, and we can't take it anymore . . . They've fucked everything up at the Detention Center. They can't get it through their skulls that the clowns we drag in without papers *never* say where they come from, so we can't deport them. They do their eight days while giving us the finger and then we let them go; it's the law."

"So why aren't *I* entitled to eight days?"

"The only guy they could find to repatriate, before you, was some Negro from Basse-Terre. They'd already bought his ticket. Then someone reminded them Guadeloupe belongs to France. You get the picture?"

I got the picture, but it was their problem. I was from Marseilles, in my heart, accent, and birth—in any case, I had the benefit of doubt, and if they brought me back anywhere, it should be to the Frioune bend: my country was the Bouches-du-Rhône, my city Floral Valley, and my home team the Olympiques de Marseille.

Pignol let out a long sigh that punctured my defense: "You're the first foreigner who actually has papers, Aziz, and who comes from somewhere."

"And what if I told them they were fakes?"

"To get what? Two years in Baumettes for using forged papers and jewelry theft? Does it really mean that much to you to be French?"

He looked at me with eyes in which our friendship appeared one last time, to say goodbye. He clearly thought that my departure was the chance of a lifetime. Nothing was keeping me here, I had no future; it wasn't doing me any good to stay. Over there I could start a new life, with the help of a specialized aide. He squeezed my knee, very tight, and said, "I'm going to miss you."

I was already gone, in his head. It's crazy how quickly people get used to things.

He walked out without turning around, dropping the little ball of chewing gum that rolled over to my foot.

There was the sound of a typewriter. Then they gave me a comb, to prepare me for what they called the preliminary interview. It was so filthy that I combed my hair with my fingers, and besides I didn't see how this could affect my fate.

And I found myself standing before the humanitarian attaché. He was a guy of around thirty-five, blond, hollow cheeks, pale skin, red eyes, glasses; not ugly but not quite finished, with the pinched mouth of people who think they really belong somewhere else. He was wearing a gray suit too heavy for here, and a funeral tie over a green-striped shirt. He held out his hand without looking at me and said, "Jean-Pierre Schneider."

I simply answered hello, because he had my name right there in front of him, on my passport. He told me to sit down but there wasn't a chair, which he didn't seem to have noticed. He was studying a map of Morocco spread out before him.

"So where are you from, exactly?"

He seemed in a hurry, even though our airplane didn't leave until the next day. I looked upside-down at my passport, for the name of the city Place Vendôme had decided I was born in.

"Irghiz," I said.

He answered, "I know, I read that, but I can't find it. Where is it?"

I understood why his eyes were red when I saw the magnifying glass on the map of Morocco. He had explored every name in the country without success. I almost told him to go ask Place Vendôme, but he no longer existed: he was no more than a twisted fork and I'd brushed him from my memory. Besides, Irghiz was surely a name he'd invented: it avoided verifications at the town hall. The attaché looked at the clock every ten seconds, as if he had another meeting after me. And, from his way of pulling at his sleeves to give his shoulders more definition, I sensed it was with a woman. I, too, had that anxiety in my muscles when I went to wait for Lila at the Niolon station, because you never know in advance what mood she'll be in, if she'll be frowning or laughing spontaneously, and you reassure yourself the best you can.

He insisted, looking stubborn:

"What is that, Irghiz? A town? A village? Where is it?"

I thought of the woman who was waiting for him somewhere. He was lucky, even if, judging by the look on his face, things weren't going so well between them. No one was waiting for *me* anymore.

"One more time: where is it?"

"Over there," I said, pointing to a corner of the map from a distance, haphazardly.

"In the Atlas Mountains?" he said, looking panicked. "Are you sure?"

"Sure I'm sure," I said, miffed.

It was an old reflex, in spite of myself. But the word *Atlas*, which had come to his lips as if by magic, as if he'd read it in my thoughts, this name that meant something to him had suddenly sucked me into the colors of his map, like the water lily that drags the swimmer to the bottom of the pond. For dozens of hours I'd been thinking of nothing but *Legends of the World*, because even though I'd lost Lila, I knew someone else would take her in his arms under the

UCPA climbing rock, while my atlas would be sold for twenty francs to a used book dealer and no one would ever have the same relationship with it that I'd had.

"Which part of the Atlas?" the humanitarian attaché asked, after looking at his watch with irritation.

I said curtly that we'd see later on; I was in a daydream. He didn't react. It gave me an odd feeling, all of a sudden, because when you got down to it he was working for me. He explained his question.

"You understand, my mission is at once specific and very vague. I have to bring you back to your place of origin, help you reestablish your roots, work with the local authorities to help find you a job . . . But the truth is, I work in public relations at the Quai d'Orsay, and they pulled me off my regular post to give me this one, which was just created. To be honest, I've had a hard time getting used to it. I'm sorry it had to fall on you."

I said me too, to be polite. I hadn't understood a word he'd said, but I found him likable enough because he was like me: his thoughts were on something else as he spoke. And besides, he had a weird accent, which didn't fit his office demeanor, something rough and hollow, with clicking consonants and vowels sunk in his throat. I found out later it was a Lorraine accent, and that he thought he'd managed to lose it.

I looked at him, hands behind my back, and tried to imagine the woman in his heart to forget about the indifference shown by Lila, who hadn't even come to see me.

He asked Pignol if he could call Paris. With a coldness I'd never seen in him before, Pignol stated that normally they weren't allowed to call outside the region because of budgetary constraints, but that he'd go ask the operator if they could reconnect the long-distance line, if the Attaché would kindly give him the number and sign and date a requisition form. The attaché answered that it wasn't important, it could wait, but his eyes said the opposite and his fingers drummed nervously on the tabletop. He let out a sigh like a door slamming, then bent back over the map of Morocco.

"All right, so it's in the Atlas, but which part? Anti, Middle, or High?"

I picked one at random, or maybe out of pride: "High."

"But that's no good at all!" he protested, tapping on a fold. "They had me get tickets for Rabat, it's at the other end of the country!"

"It's for the layout," a guy next to him said. "There's only one morning flight, and that's Rabat. The others left too late to make deadline."

He was a redhead wearing a cap. I hadn't noticed him right off because of his camera. Each time I used to go say hello to Pignol, I came across photographers for the *Provençal* and the *Méridional*, the two biggest Marseilles dailies; they're politically opposed but they belong to the same owner, and it's especially when it comes to photos that things get a bit rough, to get there first for the human interest stories and police blotter. But today's redhead wasn't a local; he had the kind of Parisian accent you hear on TV. As I was looking at him to try to find something to be vaguely interested in, the attaché introduced us. His name was Greg Thibaudot and he worked for *Paris-Match*, the magazine I read in the clinic when I have a toothache.

"He's the one doing the story," the attaché added with a sigh.

No doubt about it, my case was getting bigger all the time, and I could tell the cops had gained more respect for me in the last hour. The fat guy with a mustache had gone so far as to offer me a cigarette, even though I don't smoke, and I'd smoked it and pretended to like it to encourage the friendly atmosphere.

"The story?" I asked.

Then the attaché pushed his glasses up into his frizzy blond hair, pinched his nose between his joined hands, and sucked a gallon of air into his mouth before letting out in one burst:

"The policy of the French state is to preserve the rights of immigrant workers insofar of course as they have a job and legal status, but for the others like you we can no longer employ exclusionary means or simple repressive tactics, which are unworthy of a democracy. I'm telling you this so that everything will be crystal clear, all right?"

"Yes," I said.

"So, without going into details, the government is initiating a program that not only is in keeping with a new context of dignity, but aspires to be effective in its results, for the ultimate goal is not to make you leave a territory to which we brought you when we needed you, but rather to show you, with all the necessary assistance, that it's *your* country that needs you, for the only way to staunch the migratory flow coming from the Maghreb is to build you a future *at home*, via policies that truly incite development in both industry and human resources, and . . ."

He stopped suddenly, as if he had wound down. He turned away, swallowed his saliva, sighed heavily, and, for the first time since we'd met, looked me straight in the eye: ". . . and on Saturday, a broadcast called *Marseilles: An Arab City* pulled a thirty percent ratings share, so this is where we're launching the operation!" he threw at me in a hostile voice, as if it were my fault. "I didn't even have time to read your file! I don't even know what field you're in!"

"Car radios," I said, in spite of myself.

He looked at me for a moment, trying to regain his composure, with a gesture toward the map of Morocco to excuse his fit of temper. Then he came out with a sentence, something about zones of influence, media investments, and building a Renault plant just outside Casablanca. I nodded. It was like he was taking an exam right there in front of me.

"And would you like to continue in this profession, or would you rather be trained in something else, something perhaps better suited to your particular skills? Please don't hesitate if that's the case: I have been mandated by Foreign Affairs in cooperation with your government to simplify your administrative procedures."

"Lighting's all set," said the photographer.

"Good," said the attaché.

And he circled the table, with a constrained look on his face, to come stand next to me and rest a hand on my shoulder. And then he removed it, because it might have seemed a bit too much, and he contented himself with remaining standing, smile fixed, hands behind his back. The photographer asked me to look at the camera and not the attaché, and to smile too.

"But not too much."

I played down my smile.

"A little, all the same, but more of a puzzled smile, if you can."

I tried to look puzzled, and it wasn't very hard.

"Not too puzzled, but a little more smile. Human, if you know what I mean. With a hint of anxiety, because, you know. There! Okay, don't move now! Great—no, lose the teeth, there you go . . . Wait, yeah, keep your head like that, that's good, it looks natural. And the map, okay, you, there, I like that, that's super, you take the map of the country, show him a corner, and you, you answer him. Make like you're interested, that's it, terrific! Okay. Once more in black and white and we're done."

And things were buzzing around us, it was almost festive; I thought of my engagement banquet and the last photos must have been a bit sadder. The photographer

packed away his equipment and left us saying see you tomorrow. The attaché told me I could stop smiling now.
He looked kind of sorry.

"I must ask you to forgive me for . . . all these extras, but
the government needs them these days . . . You understand. Can I call you Ahmid?"

I said sure, for all I cared, but Pignol, who was white
with suppressed rage, retorted sharply that my name was
Aziz. The attaché begged my pardon, and what *was* he
thinking—for that last part I had my suspicions, but we
didn't know each other well enough for me to ask him the
name of the woman in his thoughts, and what she was like,
even though it would have helped pass the time. I liked
this fellow, though I couldn't figure out why. Maybe it was
the circumstances. Or the fact that he came from somewhere else.

He left without shaking my hand—he must have thought
once was enough—and said in a language that must have
been mine a word that probably meant goodbye. He shut
the door behind him without hurrying, and yet I could tell
he was running late. I hoped his wife was waiting for him
by the phone, and that their problems would all be solved
by tomorrow at the airport.

"It's disgusting," Pignol groused while bringing me back
to my cell.

"What is?" I asked.

"The whole thing! That . . . that charade, the photos,
it's really disgusting. Don't you think?"

I said no. What was disgusting, from my point of view, was the whole business about the ring. The rest was kind of sweet.

"Listen, Aziz, you're not going to play along with them, are you?"

I couldn't understand why he'd changed his tune from before. He had advised me to leave, I was leaving—what was the problem?

"But that guy's a wimp, can't you see? How do you expect him to find you a job in Morocco? He's here to get his picture snapped and that's all. He's useless!"

Something strange was going on in my head. I sensed he was right, and yet I felt I should defend my attaché. A relationship had begun between us in which Pignol had no place, and maybe that's why he was jealous.

"No, I thought he was pretty nice. We got along fine."

"Stand up for yourself for once in your life, for fuck's sake! Fight back!"

It was odd to see a policeman, even if he was my buddy, telling me to fight back against the law from behind the bars of the cage he'd just shut me into.

"Do you know why they picked you to kick out, do you get it now? It's 'cause you're good-looking, that's all. You're photogenic. Photo*genic*!"

I couldn't understand his anger. It was almost flattering.

"Cut it out, Aziz. It's making me puke! They don't know what else to do, between the unemployment and the opinion polls, so they send an Arab back where he came from, and since they just happened to pick one who looks more Corsican than Arab, that way it's less racist! And if you're happy with it all to boot. . ."

Without giving in to Arab pride, I didn't think I looked Corsican at all. But I didn't protest because Pignol had some Corsican blood from his mother, and for him it was a compliment.

"I'm not happy about it," I said, "but it doesn't bother me either."

"It doesn't bother you? All the hypocrisy, the bullshit, the PR operation they're mounting on your back, none of that bothers you?"

I shrugged modestly. He screamed that I didn't have any balls, and then he stopped himself, because it was the tone of our old arguments about soccer in the school playground, back when he and I were equals. Two fourth graders, two fifth graders, two 6-B's—only the labels on our notebooks changed from year to the year, but that was in the past, more than just in the past because of the airplane I was about to take.

"You're my pal, Aziz."

"Me too."

"It pisses me off you're leaving."

"Me too," I repeated.

But that was already less true. He lowered his eyes, turned the key, then held out through the bars a stick of gum that I didn't take. I smiled at him, nodding. It's good to have had a pal. It's less painful when they leave you than with a woman. You can keep the hope that you'll stay pals, and that the moments you've spent together won't be erased by new memories with someone else.

It was later that afternoon that Lila came to see me, with her brother Mateo—and that told me everything. She kept her eyes lowered while he talked. He told me I was a dead dog on the side of the road, which was an expression of theirs, and that to give a Manouche girl a stolen ring was the worst thing you could do, the supreme insult to the Saintes-Maries, and that he'd always said I was a shiftless Arab and a gadjo scum who didn't believe in anything. In fact, he'd brought Lila just to show her the error of her ways: it was a good thing for her I was in the hole, he said, it made her a little less dishonored that I was no longer in circulation, but it was a lesson she must never forget.

While watching him talk, I thought that it was an especially good deal for them: he kept my twelve Pioneer DVDs and forty Bose speakers as damages, while Place Vendôme would resell my ring, and to top it off the police thanked them for handing over someone so photogenic.

Lila filed out behind her brother, without having once opened her mouth. He had forbidden her from saying a word, that much I understood, but she could have said goodbye with her eyes; after all, we'd known each other a long time. My heart was in shreds. At this point I was eager to be far away, to go back where I didn't come from, to discover something new. Floral Valley and the gypsies were finished for me, and I was even looking forward to seeing the nervous fellow they'd attached to me, because he, at least, had nothing against me, he hadn't singled me out. We were two victims sent to the devil, and if that week it so happened there were no wars, deaths, or princesses, they'd put us on the cover of *Paris-Match*—but I really didn't give a damn, because there was no one left to save the clipping.

On my mattress that no longer smelled quite so bad—I'd gotten used to it, or else I'd already taken off in my head—I dreamed that the plane was going to touch down on a photo from my atlas, and the more we descended, the more real it looked, and we landed in reality, with phrases from the captions that had become the airport outbuildings. And I said to the humanitarian attaché, "Welcome to my country." He smiled and nodded his head. He looked less nervous, in my dream.

3

At nine in the morning, they gave me coffee and a biscuit and drove me to the airport. The humanitarian attaché was pacing back and forth by the departure gate, surrounded by portable barriers and airport police who ordered people to keep moving. As soon as I set foot on the sidewalk, he pulled me by the arm, telling me to hurry up, and asked where my luggage was. I answered that they'd picked my house clean, so he suggested I go get whatever I needed at the Rodier shop. I thanked him for his consideration, but pointed out that I didn't have any money. He said everything was covered by his expense account, and he gave me three thousand francs to buy some everyday clothes, but do it quick because some problems had come up—I got the feeling that was often the case with him.

In the dressing room, it was a relief to take off my white engagement suit, which was now a bad memory, soiled by prison. I bought myself (I tried haggling but it got me nowhere) a very handsome checked suit in 100 percent cotton, a shirt with purple stripes, and a matching tie. The attaché stood near the glass door of the shop with a large guy in light beige who looked like some kind of big deal, and who he introduced as the superintendent's special envoy. I understood from their looks that my suit was maybe a bit too stylish for the photos, even though I'd bought it out of respect for them—and in any case, the light beige said there wouldn't be any photos because of the turn of events. And it's true that something smelled fishy in the departure hall, but since I was taking an airplane for the first time, I tried not to look amazed.

"Right up to the end they're being a pain in the ass with this port!" groused the superintendent's envoy.

"I have to make a call," answered the humanitarian attaché. "I'll just be two minutes."

He asked the other man to watch me and disappeared toward the phone booths, while the police set up barriers to separate the travelers from the protesters arriving in greater and greater numbers.

"Mari-gnane-is-with-us!" chanted the cannery guys beneath their banners, emptying vats of bouillabaisse onto the ground.

"South Marine will survive!" blared a loudspeaker.

"You really picked the perfect day," light beige spat at me bitterly.

I told him I hadn't picked anything at all, and asked him if the airplanes were still taking off.

"That'll do, okay?" he interrupted sharply.

Behind the TV cameras that had just arrived in the ruckus, immediately encircled by the portable barriers, I spotted the photographers from the *Provençal* and the *Méridional* who were trying to elbow their way through to shoot the same thing: the dock workers' delegate attempting to rip the mike from the hands of a reporter. Lying flat on his belly on a ticket counter, the guy from *Paris-Match* was zooming in on the row of national guards who were lowering the visors of their helmets, in front of shops that were lowering their metal shutters. I could see I no longer made the grade: the report on my gentle expulsion would be replaced by the truncheoning of the angry dock workers, who had come to occupy the airport in an attempt to keep their port independent. They were more photogenic than I was.

"Out of order," said Jean-Pierre Schneider, pulling me away. "I'll try on the other side."

And we headed toward the passport control, while the loudspeakers blared that Marseilles your port is *strong*, and the naval shipyard employees chanted in chorus, "We're with you, South Marine!" while advancing in tight ranks beneath their banners, toward the forces of order who were just waiting for the cameramen to beat it.

Things were calmer in the departure lounge. I sat on a metal bench while the attaché went to try the phones. The protesters' chant was stuck in my head like a regret, a way to share their solidarity, to keep our port from dying. But I had no illusions: even if they saved the port, I would never again call it "ours." Panic doesn't always come when you expect it. The tears that had not fallen for Lila stung my cheeks at the memory of the old docks and cranes frozen in the sunset, when the gulls headed up into the harbor toward L'Estaque. Did they even have gulls on the other side of the ocean?

They boarded us by batches of numbers through a kind of bent corridor that led to the runway. The attaché, who still hadn't managed to reach his wife, nervously swung his carry-on. I imitated him with my Rodier airport bag, into which I'd finally folded my engagement suit; a memory, even a cruel one, is always worth saving.

I had thought to cross the runway filling my nose with the smells of my city, that mix of hot oil and lavender, with a hint of rotten egg wafting off the Etang de Berre, but the corridor was attached directly to the plane—and so much the better, perhaps, to keep the farewells short. When you leave for the first time, you don't know how to turn back.

And so I focused my interest on the Airbus, which had the advantage of being new for me, even if the way of entering it reminded me of the paddy wagon. Show your number, get moving, sit over there, and no smoking. The stewardesses were old, and no room for your legs. Squeezed between the seat rest in front of me and the knees of the guy in back jutting into my kidneys, I was pretty disappointed, because the planes you saw in the movies, especially *Emmanuelle*, were something else entirely. But it's true I wasn't on vacation.

The attaché suddenly stood up, stepped over my legs. He said he was going to try calling again and he'd be back. I hoped so, because without him there to guide me, I had no idea what I was going to do in my country. While waiting for him, so as not to think too much, I played with my fold-down tray. A stewardess came by and told me to cut it out, and to put my seat in the upright position for takeoff. Then a guy from the other side of the aisle shouted out that she had the wrong plane: on this one the seat backs were fixed and he had it up to here with delays and never any explanations; she answered that he wasn't supposed to be smoking, he advised her to mind her own goddamn business and the other people said they agreed, so then she retorted that *she* was just doing her job, Sir; they answered that *they* were on vacation and it wasn't so they could be treated like niggers, and it seemed to me that the ambiance on Air France wasn't all that great.

When my attaché returned, he seemed even more nervous and worn out than before. Maybe his call had gotten through. He sat back down, grinding his teeth on his troubles. Then he got up and told me in a harsh voice to take the window seat so that I could at least see the scenery, and I obliged to make him happy, but I didn't understand why he was being hostile about it. He took out an electronic game that must have served as his appointment book, absorbing himself in his schedule over the past few months to forget my presence. For my part, I was in a hurry to leave France; I told myself that a little change of scenery would do him good.

I was very afraid at takeoff, but I didn't show it. You can tell yourself all you want that the pilot knows what he's doing, you're still leaving solid ground, and after that, *inch'Allah*. The expression left a strange aftertaste: it had come spontaneously, like a reflex. It was already the atmosphere of the new country.

I busied myself with the instructions in case of accident, to avoid looking at Marseilles from above: it wasn't the last image I wanted to keep. The demonstration in the departure area was fine by me; it summarized everything I was carrying in my heart: broken promises, protest with no illusions, the indifference of outsiders. I didn't know if a new life awaited me, but my old one was dead—that was something hopeful, at least.

When the little bulbs that told us to keep our seatbelts fastened went out with a musical note, and the stewardess came back pulling the string on a deflated buoy that she'd put around her neck, Jean-Pierre Schneider folded down his tray. I didn't dare warn him that it was illegal and that the stewardess was going to yell at him. A humanitarian attaché, after all, ranks above a stewardess. He began working on my file and didn't say anything. I pretended to sleep so as not to disturb him.

When I woke up, we were still in the clouds and the pilot was saying that the weather in Rabat was sunny. I looked at the attaché, who had closed my file and was writing a letter with large angry strokes. It began with "Clementine," which was the loveliest woman's name one could imagine, but I didn't dare say so; it wasn't my place. Still, as he was crossing everything out, I allowed myself a peek. It was meant to be thrown out anyway, so there was less indiscretion. It read, "Clementine, I know you (crossed out) yet something in me (crossed out) and your voice (crossed out) give me a chance (crossed out) tell you (crossed out)."

He met my gaze and quickly covered his paper. "Don't be shy!"

"Sorry," I said. "I wasn't reading. I was just looking."

"You have a window!"

I glued my nose to the window and looked out at the sky, but I could hear him ripping up his sheet and folding his tray back up. In the passing clouds, I tried to find a face that could be right for his Clementine.

"Forgive me, Aziz. I'm a bit on edge."

I made no comment. He resumed after a moment, "I'm going through a divorce. I'd rather not talk about it."

I said fine, no problem—well, yes, it was, probably, but I understood it was personal. I almost told him about my engagement banquet, so he'd know he wasn't alone in suffering, but he came from a different background and the two stories probably had nothing in common.

"Her name is Clementine," the attaché said with a sigh.

I feigned surprise, and then I congratulated him for the lovely name. I said that basically it was like the fruit, and that Morocco was the land of clementines. But it was just for something to say; I wasn't even sure it was true. He suddenly struck the armrest separating us, which caused the overstuffed ashtray to flip open and a cigarette butt to fly out and land on my knee, and I mentioned to the stewardess who was passing by with her sour face that I didn't smoke: it was the ashtray.

"I don't understand. I don't understand what's happened to us, and *how* it could have happened!" the attaché fumed all by himself, his hands fanned out, taking the seat in front of him as witness.

He must have been talking about his problems with Clementine. I thought that things often happen on their own, and there's nothing you can do about it. The other morning I was happily sipping my engagement cocktails, and today I was the model illegal alien, the ideal deportee flying toward the country of his false ID papers, next to a man who couldn't understand why his wife had fallen out of love with him. They had chosen us at random, one for the other, but as it turned out we resembled each other. It was like our little revenge.

On the other side of the aisle, a female passenger was baring her left breast for her baby's feeding, and suddenly

Lila's absence hurt terribly. She was the most beautiful girl I'd ever known, even if she was also the only one. She came back into my arms, beneath the UCPA climbing rock, when I slid my hands under her bathing suit. I opened my eyes to erase the image. The woman across the way was blond and sweet-looking, a little like Clementine, and married to an Arab who smiled at me because he must have thought Jean-Pierre Schneider and I were a couple, since he was also blond, so that gave us a point in common.

"Have you got any children, attaché?"

He shrugged his shoulders. I realized, from his hard expression and his jaw thrust forward, that seeing the baby across the aisle bothered him as much as it did me. He took out a cigarette that he stared at fixedly before shoving it brutally back into the pack, crushing the others, and he suddenly turned toward me:

"So what did they think? That I was going to make a scene, keep them from seeing each other? Don't tell me they were worried! I was very clear: the day she told me she had someone, I left! I packed my bags, my laptop, and I went to a hotel. There! What else could I do?"

"I don't know," I said in a sorry voice.

"I should have fought back, right? Counterattacked, hired a private detective, caught them on film, file for divorce first, thrown my resignation in Loupiac's face, is that it?"

I answered that in life you don't always have time to react, and one had one's pride.

"That's her lover—Loupiac. The deputy director of PR at the ministry. He had me sent on this mission to get me out of the way. You see, I'm telling you everything."

I thanked him. We really were alike, he and I, and in the same situation—except that *he* still believed we were heading for an actual place.

"The whole thing is disgusting," he concluded in a resigned voice. "Anyway."

He again pulled out the file on which my name was written in reverse order, Kemal Aziz, like in school. The smell of ink and notebook protectors replaced Lila's body in my regrets. With an attempt at enthusiasm, the way people try to forget their woes by switching on a soccer game, he blurted out, "Let's get back to you, Aziz."

I had trouble recognizing my name in his mouth. It was sharp, truncated, harsh. Even among the gypsies, I had always heard "A-*zi*-zuh." Marseilles was already so far away. I wondered how long it would take me to lose my accent. He added, "I apologize for inflicting my moods on you."

I said there was no harm done, on the contrary: personally, I'd rather we kept talking about him, that he kept me dreaming about his Clementine from the wealthy neighborhoods, whom I saw as more and more blond and with short hair; the opposite of Lila. But I didn't have enough background to imagine their life.

"Where are you from, Mr. Attaché?"

"You can be informal with me, like in your country. It doesn't bother me."

I didn't dare answer that it bothered *me* that he was being informal. I had such pleasant memories of my six months of sixth grade, where for the first time people had spoken to me like an adult—but he took on a more formal tone of his own accord after a moment, and he was clearly more comfortable with it. Still, he added that instead of "Mr. Attaché," I could call him "Mr. Schneider," or just "Jean-Pierre," and that he lived on Boulevard Malesherbes, or at least his and his wife's home was there, so it didn't really mean anything since it was now his wife's apartment alone.

"I'm like you, Aziz, to a degree."

He was pensive for a few moments, maybe because he didn't know how to express what that degree was, and I kept silent so as not to interrupt his thoughts. There was something of the schoolteacher about this man, and it made me feel good. It reminded me of the Emile Ollivier school, where my life, no matter what they say, stopped for the first time the day I quit my classes. It felt like I was coming back from a holiday, a major holiday that had lasted seven years.

After a moment of silence, the attaché took up my file again to study my case, and I wondered why bother, since he had me right there next to him, in the flesh. He sighed.

"You know, apart from my personal situation and the interference that, well . . . I really disapprove of these methods. Not necessarily the spirit behind them, mind you; any humanitarian mission is a respectable thing, I'm not the cynical type, but all this hurry . . . First of all, I've

been working for months on the crucial matter of French-
language use in Vietnam, for the books and literature department. Nothing to do with you, of course, but then they
wonder why our foreign policy has such a terrible image.
I'm going through an emotional crisis, I absolutely should
not be budging from Paris, and there's no way I can get you
settled in two days, even without my personal problems. I'm
very sorry to put you through them, but you see what condi-
tions I was appointed under, regardless of Loupiac's med-
dling. The media really make us jump through hoops—I'm
not talking about you . . . But I didn't have any time to
prepare. And I don't even know Morocco."

Great—we were really getting off to a good start.

"Do you have a photo?" I asked.

"A photo?"

"A photo of Mrs. Schneider. I'll show you Lila, she's my
fiancée; she just left me."

He hesitated, one eyebrow suspended above his glasses,
then took a tiny ID photo hidden behind his credit cards
from his wallet. He held it out to me the way you lend
someone your bottle of water, unwillingly, because of germs.
I looked at it and immediately decided to hide my disap-
pointment: she was ugly and she had cold eyes, a pinched
mouth, heavy chin, and was completely dark. What he
needed was a blonde. I looked again at the girl across the
aisle, but differently, because I no longer needed her to
imagine Clementine, which was a ridiculous name, like
"Orange" or "Banana."

The blond caught my eye. I smiled at her, politely, and she smiled back without intention, the way people yawn when they see others yawn, but her husband decided it was enough: he took the baby from her hands to make it clear that it was his, and the breast went back into her bra. Then I pulled Lila from the pocket of my wrinkled engagement suit in the bag. The attaché said she was very beautiful, gave me back the photo, and I tore it up. Just like that, instinctively, out of solidarity, staring him in the eye. He looked at me with great hesitation, and then he tried to smile, but his lips were trembling, and he tore Clementine in half—but I could see it was just for my benefit, because he stuffed the two halves in his pocket.

And he said to me, with the authority of a gym coach, now that we were once more just among men, "Tell me about Irghiz."

I repeated his order in a questioning tone, to give myself time to come up with an answer, and I would really have preferred that we keep talking about him—but after all, I was the reason for this trip. Then I don't know what came over me. The Emile Ollivier school running through my head, with its caved-in doors, graffitied walls, brawls between classes, syringes in the hallways, and Mr. Giraudy in the middle of it all, getting old and content to be old because the spectacle was such a shame and so sad for someone like him who came from elsewhere—in short, I thought so strongly of my lost atlas, my departure gift, that I found myself telling stories in spite of myself. The words came slowly, at first falteringly, and then little by little I became more assured. It was the legend of the gray men, in Chapter 12, who lived in an utterly secret valley without roads and without progress, a green paradise with prehistoric flowers that still grew in the shelter of the bare mountains that tourists visited. But they had no idea of the valley, because the gray men swore an oath to keep the secret from generation to generation; besides, no one ever left, apart from the guards whose job it was to throw explorers off the track and keep us from being discovered. I had reworked the story of "Firdaws al m'fkoud," the lost paradise, that took place during the prophet Mohammed's flight to Medina. My secret valley was called Irghiz and I was the first of the gray men ever to leave to go to Marseilles.

The attaché listened with eyes like saucers. "But why?" he asked in a hollow voice, and I could tell that if he had been a gray man, he would never have left the valley.

I snatched at a passing image: "Because the valley is being destroyed by the new road they're building through the mountain, right, so then I left to come look for help."

He didn't hear the stewardess offering him orange juice. She left with a shrug of her shoulders. I would have loved some orange juice, my mouth was completely dry, but maybe it was only for French people, since this was an Air France flight. I said angrily, "Nobody gives a damn about Irghiz. For good reason: no one knows about it. That's why it's stayed the most beautiful place in the world, but we have to save it."

"But, why didn't you tell all this to the guy from *Match*?" Jean-Pierre cried out.

I answered that it was a secret, and that I'd already given too much away—the legend in my atlas stopped there. I wondered why I'd chosen that particular legend rather than another. It really wasn't the most useful. But it's true that it got the imagination going: you only needed to see the attaché's face.

"So then . . . *that's* where I have to take you?"

There was panic in his voice, and at the same time a childlike excitement that made me happy. One of the things I'd promised myself, beneath the UCPA rock, was to have children with Lila when she became a widow, so that I could tell them my legends and they would believe them, instead of going to swipe handbags on the sidewalk at age ten—the education we'd received. Since it's always reality that wins out anyway, it's better to let it come as late as possible.

"Wait, wait," said the attaché, loosening his tie, "I don't follow you. Why go to Marseilles? You left a valley that's cut off from the rest of the world and went to *Marseilles*?"

I knew perfectly well that my story didn't hold water. So I said that an elder knew a professor from the University of Marseilles, Mr. Giraudy, who had a solution to keep the valley from crumbling, and my mission had been to convince Mr. Giraudy to come help us with his team.

"But how did the elder know this professor if he'd never left the valley?"

He was starting to get on my nerves. A legend isn't something you analyze; it's something you listen to. But then again, for him, this was reality. I was pretty amazed that he'd believed me so easily. Maybe he was putting himself in my place, and with his intelligence he couldn't imagine I would tell a gratuitous lie, when he was here at my service to find me a home in a zone of influence. My interest was to open doors for myself with his ministerial prestige, so I had no reason to pull him into a fantasy where I had nothing to gain.

"By helicopter," I said.

"By helicopter?"

"Yes. Mr. Giraudy had come by helicopter to explore the mountain, and he crashed in the village. So then we treated him with magic herbs, and he said to us, 'I am a professor at the University of Marseilles, specializing in the mysteries of the earth. If you ever need anything, come see me, because I owe you my life.' And he pledged complete secrecy when he left."

I was glad to give some extra play to Mr. Giraudy, my old geography teacher, to make him out as a kind of Indiana Jones. He deserved it.

"Except that now," the attaché got revved up, "we have to let the whole world know that the gray men exist, to create a chain of solidarity and save the valley! Is that it? You really are something else! When I think that we had that guy from *Match* right there in our hands—we could have taken him with us, it would have made an incredible article. I would have been reinstating you as an ecological militant, the savior of Irghiz, France helping Morocco protect an archeological treasure! But that's all right, we've still got time, we can make it for the next issue and I'll get a TV station on the case. Do they have phones?"

"Where's that?"

"In Irghiz."

And it struck me as so funny to see that he was already at home in my legend, it struck me as so funny that, just like that, he became my pal. He became "Schneider," as before I used to say "Pignol," because it's normal that friends evolve in life: up to this point I'd dabbled in car radios and protected a cop. Now I was speeding through the clouds toward an unknown land where I'd planted my legend in place of roots, and I was protecting an intellectual who needed to dream to forget his wife.

When I stopped laughing, I could see his feelings were hurt. The guy had heart, despite his office life and emotional crises, and he felt ashamed with his telephone because I was telling him of a paradise where real human relations must have existed, and perhaps over there, in a grotto near a spring, cut off from the world, he might not have lost his Clementine. And I could easily guess his moral dilemma: should he save Irghiz by turning it into a Club Med, or let the mountain swallow up its beauty without ever spoiling it?

I had come across a movie like that once, by mistake. Lila and I had gone to see *Terminator* in a cineplex, and with all those hallways we ended up in the wrong theater. We had found ourselves in a kind of long cellar where they were showing a documentary on Rome. It was so strange that we stayed a while. There was a scene where the guys digging the subway tunnels discovered a cavern filled with prehistoric paintings. There they were, stock still, staring in awe, and meanwhile the paintings had started fading away because of them, because of the oxygen they had let in. Jean-Pierre, too, felt guilty: before even knowing it, he was blaming himself for the harm he was going to cause my valley.

I turned the button on the air flow above my head. How crazy the power of a legend was when someone took the trouble to believe in it. In the end, my attaché was more competent than he thought. In less than an hour, he had already set up my new life: I was an Arab storyteller.

Jean-Pierre tightened his tie against the cold air I'd released, then, as I shut it off, he knitted his brows and turned a little more toward me in his seat. "But, Aziz . . . You told me you worked with car radios . . ."

"I didn't work with them. I swiped them."

That bit of candor had popped out of me without my permission. I regretted the faux pas when I noticed that this type of sincerity, against my own better interests, lent even more truth to Irghiz. I was becoming a damn good storyteller. Schneider, after a moment of surprise, brushed away my confession like a fly: "That's none of my business. I don't want to know anything about your past as an illegal alien, your time in Marseilles. None of that counts for me, I'm not the police. What I'm interested in is Irghiz. Your roots and your future."

My eyes drifted back to the blonde who had taken her breast out again, and seeing the child suckling made me sad: *she* was building her future, in a way, while I was nursing a legend that was about to suffer a miscarriage the moment we landed in Morocco and Jean-Pierre asked me for directions—I mean, I wasn't going to run him around for a month looking for a junk valley so that everyone could laugh at him in my country and his bosses could reprimand him for the wasted expense. Better to try for a smooth landing. At least we'd spent a nice moment together.

"Sir, there's something I have to tell you . . ."

"Call me Jean-Pierre."

"There's something I have to tell you, Jean-Pierre . . . Mr. Giraudy, actually, was a geography teacher at the Emile Ollivier school, that's all."

"Ah, hell," said Jean-Pierre, who looked sincerely distraught. "So you tracked him down in Marseilles, and when you realized he was leading you on a wild goose chase and wasn't the great archeologist he'd made himself out to be, you sank into . . . you found yourself with nothing, I mean. And you didn't dare return to Irghiz empty-handed."

My story really had whetted his appetite. It was hard taking the food out of his mouth, and even a bit cruel, and besides I'd become rather fond of my lost valley myself. But I had no choice. I said gently, "Mr. Schneider, Irghiz doesn't exist."

"Yes, of course, I know—secrecy, the oath. I respect your traditions, of course I do, but we have to do something. And I'm here to help."

This was starting to turn sour. On the other hand, as soon as we touched down, he'd forget about my valley to go call his wife on the phone, and I'd disappear into the woodwork without ruining his dream; it was the best thing for both of us. My path was traced, as they say: I'd swipe car radios in a new land and he'd return to his ministry to reconcile with his wife. I could tell that my legend had opened a breach in his universe, and I had no desire to be the subway worker who destroys the remnants for a little fresh air.

"Irghiz doesn't exist," I repeated.

"So what did you do there, originally?"

The guy really was thick-headed. To have done with it, I coughed up everything in no particular order: that I was a native Marseillais who'd been smashed up in an Ami 6, hence my name, and that the valley of the gray men was just a legend in the atlas Mr. Giraudy had given me the day I left school to become a lark. He smiled shrewdly, because he knew full well that earlier I'd been telling the truth about Irghiz. He asked again, "What did you do?"

I let out a sigh. He took my silence for I don't know what, but it only encouraged him. He started making suggestions: "Artisan? Farmer? Shepherd?"

I realized there was no point in trying, since my protests only reinforced his certainty. From the moment he had decided to believe in my story, all my attempts to backtrack only heightened the lure of a forbidden secret that I had betrayed without meaning to.

"Nobody works in Irghiz," I snapped. "We gather fruits, we eat the beasts of the fields, we drink from springs."

"Yes . . . please understand . . . Excuse me for clinging to these ridiculous concrete details, but to carry out my mission strictly speaking, I have to return with a document proving you've found a job in your birthplace. So fine, I understand that you'd rather say Irghiz doesn't exist and we forget about saving it, but what do I tell my superiors? It's an impasse."

I didn't say a word, because it was in fact an impasse, and it seemed to cause him intense pleasure. I had gone too far, but at the same time I was glad to see him so happy, revived, full of plans. We'd see what we'd see.

The stewardess gave us plastic trays, with different-colored mashed foods in little tubs. Jean-Pierre lifted the covering off the yellowest mash, then poured over it the contents of a tiny packet that he'd pulled from his carry-on bag. It looked like sawdust.

"They're germs," he explained, seeing my look.

I pressed back against the window, while he tore open the bag containing the silverware. Maybe he was training for chemical warfare, contaminating himself a little each day as a vaccine.

"I'm fighting an excess of free radicals. And I need selenium, for my depression. Would you like some?"

He asked so nicely that I said yes, without any real conviction. You really need to know people in life before judging them. I had left with an agitated bureaucrat and I found myself with an apprentice savior, an adventurer from the future who ate germs.

"You'll see, it's excellent and completely organic. Selenium exists in the natural state in each germ."

He opened my yellow tub and dusted it with the stuff. Then he attacked his own with the energy of an optimistic invalid. It reminded me of the Chinese mummies in my atlas, who embalmed themselves while still alive by gnawing on acorns.

"So what illness are these germs from?" I asked, fork poised, watching him devour them out of the corner of my eye.

"Excuse me?"

"Are they dangerous?"

"Dangerous? No, why? It's wheat."

I ate, a bit let down. He unscrewed my bottle of wine and filled my glass, before suddenly gulping it down and begging my pardon. Then he poured some mineral water into his own cup and handed it to me. I said thanks—I'd wait until he went to the john to ask for some more wine. You should never shock people when it comes to religion. After his yellow tub, he attacked the brown one and began to summarize the situation that he'd analyzed while chewing:

"The problem is simple. On the one hand, we have to make Irghiz exist in the eyes of the world, so that France and UNESCO will free up funds for an archeological rescue mission, and on the other hand, we have to keep the site from being overrun by tourists. That seems contradictory, but there might be a way." Then he lowered his voice, while his fingers tightened around my arm. "I'm not at all well, Aziz. I haven't been well for a long time, and it's not because of Clementine. It's much more serious. That's why I married a woman like her, knowing she'd leave me. I, too, abandoned my homeland. I renounced my origins, my upbringing. And since that day, nothing has been right."

I nodded. Whatever his story was, I felt full of compassion for him; it would distract me from my own problems. He explained, his voice breaking, that he was born in Uckange, in the Lorraine, next to a foundry. His father and brother were foundrymen, and at seventeen he had decided to cut his ties, but so that he could make something of himself: he had secretly written a novel about his father's life, and he'd gone up to Paris to have it published. But up there, the Lorraine was of no interest to anyone, and he'd had to take courses to become a number in an office. He earned a good living, sent checks to his family, but he'd never had the heart to set foot in the Lorraine again because he hadn't been able to make it come alive as a novel in Paris. And now his father was old, the foundry was shutting down, France's best metallurgic region was about to become a Smurf theme park, Clementine was leaving him because she'd married him as a future writer, and he had blown everything.

So for him, Irghiz was perhaps his last chance. It was a fabulous fictional subject, because the Lorraine didn't set any hearts racing, but in the final account the valley of the gray men was *my* Lorraine. He was putting himself in my place. He would say "I" when talking about me, could express along the way everything that was weighing on his heart, and the book would be the best way to let people know about the valley of Irghiz without ruining it. He said he believed in God, that it was no accident that Providence had put me in his path, it was fantastic, the novel started here in the Airbus, and of course he'd give me half his royalties since he'd been inspired by my story, was I comfortable with that?

I said nothing. The airplane had lowered its landing gear and, in a way, it would have been better if it had crashed. For the first time in my life I was responsible for someone. The little blond man with his glasses and his checkered suit—if I ditched him at the airport, as I'd planned to, in a land that existed only through my legend, he was done for. Given the state he was in, with the confession of my lie and the failure of his mission, despite his wheat germ for depression, he might even kill himself.

Shaking my hand, radiant, he exclaimed, "This is going to be fantastic!"

I nodded.

We found ourselves in the crowds of Rabat, which looked like the ones in Marseilles except for the color of the uniforms. I had some problems with my passport, because here, of course, it looked faker than in France. I was sort of hoping they'd send me back; honor would be preserved—we could write the novel in Paris—but Jean-Pierre pulled out a whole series of stamped papers from my file, proving that his official mission was to bring me back to my country, and therefore that I was indeed I since he was indeed he. A fax on Kingdom of Morocco letterhead confirmed the whole thing and directed the authorities to facilitate matters for the bearer of the present document. After having rectified his position, the officer said something to me in Arabic and I smiled vaguely, at which he gave me an annoyed look. I must have misjudged the tone of his sentence.

The attaché dragged me toward the phone booths. This large room full of Moroccans made me feel like I was wearing a shoddy disguise that everyone could see through: I wasn't *real*, I didn't speak the language. But it wasn't my fault if I came from Marseilles.

"We need a title," said Jean-Pierre.

"Sorry?"

"For our book. What will it be called?"

I said, *"The Humanitarian Attaché."*

It was out of modesty, and also because I didn't really see what *I* could be called in a title. He said no, his eyes shining, and he pronounced solemnly, one finger raised in the air: *"Accompanied Baggage."*

And he even stopped on his way to the telephone to taste the title on his lips, nodding his head three times.

"That's me," he explained. "Or actually, you, in the novel. The accompanied baggage. All the irony of the situation, the pathos and absurdity . . ."

I nodded too, but I wasn't quite sure how to take it. He tried calling Clementine to tell her the good news, but the line was still busy. Then he looked at his watch, the flight departure board, and asked me if, to get to Irghiz, it was shorter via Marrakech or Agadir. I said Agadir to gain time, because it was the last flight out.

We spent four hours in the airport restaurant. Jean-Pierre, between two attempted phone calls, took notes like crazy, on the backs of official papers that he pulled from my file, to create a life for himself based on mine. No sooner did I open my mouth than he filled three pages, because it suggested other, personal things to him, and that made me uncomfortable. He invited me to lunch: I had a brioche, he a couscous with *merguez* sausages that were white with congealed fat, which he lathered in *harissa* to "put himself in my skin," as he said, and to "set the stage."

I didn't know how to get out of this situation. My first idea, simply to slip away, wasn't workable anymore now that he'd decided to make a book out of my legend. It was too important, too personal for me to turn my back and just leave it to him. Something of myself was coming to life under his felt tip. And besides, his face had been transformed. Wrapped up in the words that were coming to him, he sometimes stopped to thank me, his eyes burning, and he plunged back into work with murmurs and sighs of suffering. I felt like a father watching his child being born.

Finally they announced our flight, and Jean-Pierre went back one last time to try Clementine's number. He got it. He came back looking very serious, very sad, and completely extinguished. Thirty seconds of conversation with that woman had shattered four hours of enthusiasm with me. On the other hand, he was leaving me in peace.

We got into another plane, smaller and dirtier than the first, with flower-upholstered seats and a stewardess who wasn't so old. There were no fold-down trays. My attaché, his legs crossed, leaning on his knee, started up again writing crossouts to his wife. As I felt like I was no longer anything to him, not even accompanied baggage, I closed my eyes to dream about the blonde with her left breast from the other airplane, whom I missed a bit. Maybe I'd ask Jean-Pierre to write in a love story between me and her. We'll say that her husband divorced her and took the baby, and out of sorrow she joined us on the road to Irghiz, because if not there won't be any women and nobody will buy it. And besides, one girl between two friends always becomes a problem since she loves us both, but in fact it will only strengthen our friendship. And in the final chapter, as I fall asleep against the airplane window, it will be Jean-Pierre taking the place of the infant at the blonde's breast, next to a spring surrounded by plane trees and umbrella pines, in a cave lit as if in broad daylight by shining rocks, covered in drawings etched over millions of years by the gray men of Irghiz.

4

The hotel was a big modern affair that looked like the Marseilles Sofitel. It was full of Frenchmen who were bitching and moaning because it was too hot, they were sick of waiting, and nothing looked as nice as it did in the brochure. The humanitarian attaché checked us in, asked to have his phone switched on, gave me the key to my room, and then disappeared toward his own.

My eyes remained glued to the elevator door that closed behind him. I felt strange, abandoned, unresolved, like a character in a sentence that the author hadn't bothered to finish. The Moroccan porter offered in French to carry my plastic bag, and it embarrassed me even more than earlier, when the Rabat policeman spoke to me in Arabic. I shook my head no and went up to shut myself in my room.

The room was eighteen by twenty-one—I measured with my feet. I'd never had a hotel room to myself before, and at first it felt odd. I played with the TV, the faucets, the little soaps, and that weird contraption that looked like it was for washing dogs but was actually for shining shoes, after which I got bored.

I stood for a moment on the balcony, staring at the sea, the sand, the moon, the stars, the guardrail, the floor tiles. It smelled like I don't know what, but mostly good. The air was light, almost too light; there weren't enough cars and it was too quiet. I tried telling myself that this could well be the land of my ancestors, but deep down I didn't really give a shit. All that mattered was Room 418, with that young man who was fantasizing about my legend. It was funny, because *I* was thinking about his Lorraine, his family, his foundry—I didn't have a clear picture of what a foundry was, physically, but I didn't want it to become a Smurf park. I felt a strong urge for him to tell me more about this Lorraine, even if we didn't put it in the book. I, too, wanted to "transpose," re-create a childhood for myself based on his, now that my past no longer existed.

I took a shower, dressed, put on my tie, and then went to wait at the door of Room 418. I didn't knock right away, out of tact, because just then I heard him saying that he hadn't chosen this bullshit mission, it was all Loupiac's idea. He wasn't running away from the reality of their separation by leaving with this Maghrebi, darling, and she had to understand that he loved her and that life without her was barren and that people can — can often — revive the fire of the old volcano that everyone thought was dead and that, shit, goddammit.

A pause followed these last words. Then he resumed his sentence at the part about the old volcano, and I realized he was talking to an answering machine that must have cut him off. A girl was passing by with a laundry cart, and I bent down to tie my shoelaces. He repeated that he hadn't chosen this ridiculous mission and, squatting by his door, I felt guilty that they'd attached him to me instead of letting him save his marriage, since it mattered so much to him. Still, as I was standing back up, he added that everything was about to change, because he'd started writing another book. He believed in himself again, the old volcano was going to spit fire again, he would seduce her like the first time, do you remember, Clementine, when I read you my manuscript in the university cafeteria?

I waited for the next cut-off, thirty seconds later, and knocked. He said to come in; I stuck my head in to tell him I was going out for a little walk, and not to worry. It was the least I could do: if I took off, he'd be the one held responsible. At least, that's how it seemed.

He turned a haggard face toward me. He was wearing striped pajamas, hair disheveled, looking like a jeweler at gunpoint.

"I'm going out for a little air."

He answered, "Sure . . . fine."

Then he pounced on the road map unfolded on the minibar.

"What direction are we heading in tomorrow?"

It reassured me to see that he was still attached to my valley, despite the old volcano, and I put my finger on a corner of the High Atlas where there was nothing written. What surprised me was that I had to consciously remind myself Irghiz was just a fiction.

"So what's the best way to get there?"

At my silence, he rephrased his question by asking what means of transportation I had used on the trip out. I answered that I'd started out on mule back and that it had taken three weeks, which struck me as both realistic and unverifiable. He looked at me sorrowfully, imagining all the trouble I'd been through for nothing, and then his smile slowly returned, because the misfortunes of others always make you feel better when you're down. He clapped me on the back to buck me up, booming out in a dynamic voice, "We leave at eight o'clock! I'll deal with Hertz. What do you think—Jeep, 4 x 4, or Range Rover? What kind of car should we treat ourselves to?"

I told him to get one with fold-down trays to write on, and he rested a hand on my shoulder, thanking me with his eyes. I went back out as he returned to his telephone. Before lifting the receiver, he told me not to go too far and be careful. It might have been nothing special for someone with parents, but it was the first time I'd heard that sentence.

I went out to get some air around the swimming pool. I liked it at first because everything was carefully put away for the night, chairs stacked and mats in a pile, and then I saw there were lovers kissing beneath the trees, so I went to sit in the lobby. I looked at the flyers scattered on a table to learn about Morocco but I didn't retain anything. Local customs, typical houses, land of contrasts—it wasn't for me. I was looking for roots, and they were offering excursions. I didn't recognize Irghiz in any of the suggested tourist itineraries. This secret valley that I'd created as a birthplace for myself became a weight on my heart, all the heavier because I didn't know where to locate it, in the snow or the sand, in the heat of stones or the cool of an oasis; it was fading like a mirage. I folded away the brochures and went out again.

In front of the hotel, porters were excitedly talking to each other. They lowered their voices and watched me carefully as I passed because I was from the other world, the tourist side, in my suit that still smelled of France.

A long, straight road, bordered by a mangy platform decorated with bits of gravel and dead grass, departed from the hotel toward the city. I followed it for a long time, hands behind my back. Buses passed me en route to typical meals in the medina. I knew that *medina* meant the center of town, that the market was called a *souk*, and that the religion forbade beer and ham. In any case, I wasn't hungry. I was just walking for the hell of it.

The streets started livening up, with open windows in every home, music pouring out of them, colored light bulbs in the trees, and colleagues on the sidewalks selling radios, rugs, leather jackets, jewelry, and souvenirs. Customers from the buses haggled while munching on oily pastries. Since I had nothing to sell, I didn't exist for anyone.

I felt anxious, totally isolated in the middle of all these people whom I resembled, and who spoke a language different from mine, without a Marseilles accent. For the first time in my life, I felt like an immigrant. To feel less lonely, I thought about the solitude of the Arab landing in France, especially when he's an illegal alien. I should count myself lucky to have an attaché, a bodyguard bearing a pass from the king so they wouldn't give me any trouble, a nice guy who made room for me amid all his problems, who took care of booking the hotel and renting the car, and who in return asked for nothing but a piece of my dream so he wouldn't be so alone.

At the same time, I felt like an amnesiac in a soap opera: I was walking in the midst of my origins and it didn't remind me of anything, even though it stirred something. And people jostled me without seeing me, because for them I was part of the scenery. It would make for a fine passage in the novel. In the final account, Jean-Pierre had sent me to the market to pick him up some impressions, descriptions that rang true, local scents, and my own moods.

I committed to memory the prices of two or three souvenirs, the smell of the fried dough, the colors of the houses, the height of the trees, and the makes of cars. And concentrating on these bits of information, I turned back toward the long straight road that I had already described on the way out.

In front of the hotel were two souvenir shops that sold the same items as on the street, in more fashionable versions. A bus had just pulled up, with dirty windows, exhausted people, suitcases to unload, and problems that were just beginning. It must have been one of those express tours, the Maghreb in six days, because they all wanted to buy their souvenirs before going to bed, saying that tomorrow at dawn it would be closed. The female guide promised it wouldn't, but they weren't listening. On top of which, they all wanted to go to the shop on the right, which had Vuitton on sale for a good price, and the guide could repeat until she was blue in the face that as part of Morocco Tours they would get the same deal in the shop on the left, but still they all crammed into the one on the right, to get in a few bargains behind the back of Morocco Tours, which was surely taking a cut at their expense.

Another bus had just arrived, an Oasis Travel that had made an arrangement with the shop on the right, and the people from Oasis were howling because the Morocco Tours were going to steal all the bags *they* wanted, so the Oasis guide went over to negotiate with the Morocco guide, who tried to get her charges out of the right-hand shop, swearing to them that the other one had the *same* bags for the *same* price, but the Moroccos didn't want to hear it. They said they were free citizens and they'd spent the last four hundred miles on their asses: they weren't taking orders from anybody and Oasis could just wait its turn.

As the guide was starting to lose her temper, they formed two resistance groups, one shouting, "Hoooh!" and the other chanting in demonstration rhythm, "Hey, ho! The guide must go! Hey, ho! The guide must go!" At which point, on the verge of a nervous breakdown, she started yelling, "Go fuck yourselves!"

And right at that moment, it's funny, but I knew she'd be the right woman for Jean-Pierre. She was about twenty, wearing jeans with patches on the seat, pretty, nicely rounded buttocks, a Morocco Tours T-shirt with a bra of the same color, nice-looking breasts, hair cut any which way, dirty with sweat and road dust, apparently a real blonde (though under the neon of the shops you couldn't be sure), with sunglasses planted in her scalp.

"Go on, you idiots, buy your crap so you can feel like such big shots back home! I'm sick to death of your stupid faces, you don't even look at the wonders we're trying to show you, you're a bunch of morons! You're sheep! You're vegetables! You can drive your own goddam bus, I'm getting the fuck out of here!"

She dove into the hotel to the cheers of the Oasis Travelers, who were delighted to see the Morocco Tourists humiliated. They started taking snapshots of their stunned faces, souvenir of Agadir, and the women from Morocco thundered and demanded a manager while one lone thickhead continued to chant, "Hey, ho! The guide must go!"

and the others took advantage of the situation to swipe Vuitton bags by the dozens.

In the hotel, I found the guide ordering a whiskey. The bar was painted white and decorated in minaret style, with giant fans and wicker stools. Perched on one buttock, her elbows on the counter, she downed her drink in one gulp. I went to sit next to her, told the bartender to give her another and a Coke for me. She didn't say a word, didn't turn her head. She had clapped her hands over her ears to shut everything out. Her nose was long and a little pinched, her forehead stubborn, her lips thin. Not exactly the easy-going type, clearly, but competent. She discovered my presence when the refilled glass was set in front of her and I told the bartender it was for me. She pushed the whiskey toward me. I said no, she'd misunderstood; it was for her, but I was paying: that was what I'd meant. And then I felt in my pockets, remembering I didn't have any money on me. She watched me and suggested I give up trying to learn French.

"*Baraka Allah oufik!*" she said in my direction, lifting her glass. "So, okay, no more of those morons, but now what am I going to do?"

She was putting the question to the snake that surrounded the palm tree on the tattoo decorating her arm. She paid for her two whiskeys and my Coke and left.

I caught up with her in the lobby and asked if she was free. There again I didn't make myself clear: she looked me up and down and asked if I took her for a whore — no? Then so long.

I called out, annoyed, "That's not what I meant!"

"Piss off."

I like women, but they shouldn't take advantage of the fact, and I wasn't from Morocco Tours. Which is exactly what I told her, staring her in the face, my hands gripping her elbows after I'd spun her toward me. And I explained that my friend and I needed a guide; we weren't morons, weren't interested in Vuitton bags. We were writers in transit, heading for the High Atlas, we had the means to pay for a car and a private guide, and I had chosen her: how much did she charge? Unless she'd rather go back and be lynched by the mob. And in fact, things were getting pretty ugly out there; they had just carried in two women from opposing buses who had apparently beaten each other silly, and the hotel manager was rushing up to see what the story was.

"What's your room number?" asked the guide.

Since I didn't remember, I went over to ask the receptionist. He looked in the register and handed me a key, which the girl snatched away before rushing off toward the elevators. I was a bit taken aback, but I followed her. The doors closed on us. On the other side, furious voices demanded to know where the Morocco Tour guide had disappeared to.

We both stood quietly in the rising elevator, looking away. At the fourth floor, she asked if I wouldn't mind putting her up. I said I guess not. She said that in that case I could show a little more enthusiasm.

The telephone started ringing the moment we entered the room. It was the hotel manager asking to speak with the guide. I told him that was impossible: she had just been requisitioned for an official mission by the French government. He could go over the details tomorrow with Schneider, my ministerial attaché who was carrying a pass from King Hussein, and this was no time to be pestering us. I surprised myself by hanging up on him. It's impressive how fast you can take on an air of authority when you have a little power.

"Hussein is in Jordan, Mr. Writer. The king here is Hassan. But thanks all the same."

Her voice was gentle, slow, a bit mocking. When she began removing her T-shirt, I said it wasn't necessary—I had my pride. I was perfectly happy to give her a place to stay for the night without us ending up in bed, and I'd already told her I didn't think she was a whore. She pulled her T-shirt back on and I felt like an idiot. I said well, that wasn't exactly what I'd meant either. She replied in a cutting tone that she didn't give a shit about her body, she never felt anything and I could be her guest if I felt like trying my luck, since guys seem to get off on women who can't come, as if there were some prize to be won. I said in a dignified voice that first of all I was engaged, even if, well never mind, that was my problem, and besides it wasn't my fault if she was like that and she didn't need to take that tone with me. She said she was keyed up. I said me too. She again removed her T-shirt, saying that at least it would relax us, and this time I didn't argue.

When her maroon panties fell off after rolling down her thighs, I thought that if she didn't like lovemaking, it really was an awful waste. She was standing naked before me on the rug, and I tried to open the minibar to create a little ambiance. Using the key ring as a crowbar, I ended up prying open the door and endeavored to fix us a house cocktail. Lying across the bed, cigarette dangling from her lips, she watched me mix the miniature liquors. After pointing out that, normally speaking, the key will open the minibar if you just put it in the keyhole, she asked me with a kind of hope if I was impotent. I was just preoccupied, because of Irghiz and Jean-Pierre. And then I thought to myself that, all things considered, making love to this girl would be the simplest way of explaining the whole situation to her afterward.

When I undressed and turned her over on the bed, she said whoa, hey there, we don't know each other well enough, and I answered, exactly, it was to respect her before marriage. But I was forgetting she wasn't a gypsy, so I climbed back onto her belly, looking at her face to face, and it was good, too, even if she stared at me patiently while waiting for me to finish. It left me feeling strange. Try as I might to concentrate, move in different ways, pass from delicacy to violence, it was as if I was washing her car and she was waiting behind the windshield.

"I can stop if you like."

"It doesn't matter to me," she said.

"Well, maybe it matters to me!"

"Look, if we're just going to keep fighting, let's forget it."

"I'm not the one who started!"

"So what kind of books do you write?"

I tried to mark my male superiority with a hard thrust. She replied that it wasn't an answer. So then I told her they were men's stories. That shut her up, and I was able to keep my mind on my own pleasure by thinking about Lila, who put so much heart into lovemaking that it brought tears to my eyes, which fell onto the blonde girl's breasts.

"Are you crying or is that sweat?"

I didn't answer. I swallowed back those ridiculous tears that came from a past I was trying so hard to forget, but that had made me happy nevertheless. In a way, I was glad to bury Lila in the body of this girl who didn't feel a thing. It was punishment for having betrayed me. I wondered if I'd be a sentimental fool all my life. And then she let out a cry, because without meaning to, from thrusting at her over and over, I had pushed her to the top of the bed and she had banged her head against the wall. From the other side we heard a sleepy voice answer, "Come in."

We both burst out laughing at the same time, one in the other, and I don't know what happened, maybe inner vibrations, but I think we rose to heaven together. We rolled on the sheets holding our sides, it hurt so much. We couldn't breathe. But suddenly we looked at each other with barriers down, like friends. It was better than love, and completely new. We were two strangers rejected by everyone else, and I was proud to be taking her to Irghiz.

"Bastard," she said with a smile. "That's cheating."

I murmured that my name was Aziz, so as not to linger in my modest triumph. She answered that it was almost good, which from her must have been a compliment. So I said thanks, and that I'd do better next time. She said there wouldn't be a next time. It was a matter of principle with her. The only way to have normal relations with men was to sleep with them right off the bat, that way they had what they wanted and you could move on to other things—like conversation, for instance. I was shocked, but I didn't let it show. She was obviously well educated. I asked her, and in fact she had degrees in a bunch of fields I'd never even heard of. I decided to change the subject.

"Why did you get yourself a tree tattoo?"

She said it was none of my business—a family matter. I didn't push the point. Following her into the bathroom, I asked her name.

"Valerie."

I liked that. In any case, it was more normal than Clementine.

"Valerie what?"

"D'Armeray."

"Valerie, I have to talk to you."

A silence followed. She waited, leaning on the sink. As the silence dragged on a bit, she made me leave the bathroom. I went to drink my house cocktail, which was even worse than the americanos at Café Marchelli. She called out from behind the door:

"Your offer, before—did you mean it, or was it just so you could fuck me?"

I shouted back that she really was obsessed, and that there was more to life than sex. She opened the door and told me I was sweet, and we drew ourselves a bath.

"Do you know Konrad Lorenz's work on geese?"

I had a strong feeling it had nothing to do with foie gras, so I kept my answers vague.

"I'm writing my sociology thesis on group aggression. Being a guide pays for my studies and gives me raw material. And besides, if you want to live in Morocco, it's not like you've got a million options. You want bubble bath?"

"Sure. Why don't you go back to France?"

"I was born here. And I don't want to talk about it. First of all, I don't have a choice. But no prob, I'm cool with my geese. I don't usually have breakdowns like that. That's a new one for me."

I nodded. It was new for me, too, to be soaking in the foam as a twosome after lovemaking, as friends. It was good. I kept myself from caressing her so as not to spoil the moment. Leaning against my chest, her hair in my nostrils, absently twisting the hairs on my calves, she listened to my story: the Ami 6, Floral Valley, my arrest at Café Marchelli, the expulsion for *Match*, the humanitarian attaché's wife who wanted a divorce, and the legend in the airplane. She didn't say a word. I checked three times to see if she'd fallen asleep, but no, she was following, pulling on my leg hairs to start me up again when I paused.

At the end of my story, I asked her with a lump in my throat if she would agree to help me keep up the charade for Jean-Pierre. She didn't answer right away. Her toe drew designs in the condensation on the blue ceramic tiles. She asked me to repeat precisely the description of Irghiz that I'd improvised in my Air France seat.

I closed my eyes to try to recapture the words, the valley, the cave lit by the glowing rocks around the magic spring, and the new mountain road that threatened to obliterate the gray men who had survived in secret since prehistoric times.

"I think the M'Goun range will do the trick. We'll make it one-third desert, one-third oasis, and one-third snow-covered peaks. How does that sound?"

I said great.

"And when we get halfway up the Ayachi, which sounds pretty close to what you're describing, you can tell him it's too late, an avalanche has already buried Irghiz, and I'll bring you back. You think he'll buy it?"

I answered that he wanted to so much, and needed to so much, because of the Lorraine. All the way until dawn we polished the details of our scenario, occasionally adding more hot water to the tub, and then we went to sleep together for an hour. I sensed that I'd come along at a good time for her; she'd get some of her own back by guiding someone toward a marvelous place that didn't exist. It would take her mind off her geese, tourist sites, the obligatory splendors, souvenirs on sale. We were lying naked against each other in the fresh sheets. I no longer felt desire for her; it was something else, gentler, more confident, and I told myself that I was perhaps falling in love for the second time in my life.

"You know, Valerie . . ."

"Mmmh?"

My nose in the hollow of her shoulder, I erased my thoughts in her scent.

"Nothing."

Gently pulling my hand toward her, she replied, "Don't go getting ideas."

5

I found the attaché in the lobby at ten minutes to eight. He looked like someone who hadn't slept, and he had dressed himself up like an explorer in a safari jacket, a Legionnaire's white scarf, high-top shoes, and a baseball cap. He had also bought a cell phone, with which he was now pacing back and forth.

The moment he saw me, he ran up, pulling by the arm a kind of boxer in djellaba so that he could introduce us. The boxer's name was Omar; he was a specialist in the Atlas region and had agreed to bring us there in his jeep. I pulled Jean-Pierre aside to tell him it wouldn't work. As he didn't understand my reaction, I whispered that Omar was a Razaoui, the hereditary enemy of the gray men of Irghiz, and my argument won him over: he went back to pay off the boxer, who walked away happy to have made such an easy profit.

Then I announced to Jean-Pierre that I'd found the ideal driver: a girl from a good family, native of Bordeaux, with a *de* in front of her name—well, almost: a *d'*—who I was sure he'd like and who knew the High Atlas like the back of her hand, notably the existence of the gray men, but without being able to locate the exact entrance to the valley, fortunately. As he still had a somber look on his face, I added brightly that we'd just have to blindfold her. He asked where she was, and I told him she was waiting for us on the beach. He said the answering machine was full. Seeing my disconcerted look, he pushed the antenna back into his phone, adding that all he got now was a beep, the proof that he'd used up the entire tape; now he didn't even have Clementine's voice telling him to leave a message after the tone. It was terrible for him; it meant things were really over between them. It meant silence.

"*I'm* here," I murmured.

He looked at me with a strange intensity, as if trying to figure out what part I played in his marriage; then he pulled out the antenna again while saying, "I love her."

I said to myself that things hadn't worked themselves out overnight, and that it was time for action. I led him to the porch. His hand hanging limp at the end of his arm, he dragged his telephone by the antenna like a leash you keep walking even after the dog has died. I had arranged for us to meet under an umbrella, over breakfast, so that he'd see Valerie in a bathing suit, which struck me as her most convincing argument. I was less sure about the proper language she'd promised to use—old Bordeaux family and all.

"This is Miss Valerie d'Armeray," I introduced. "And this is Jean-Pierre Schneider, my humanitarian attaché."

"How do you do?" she went, holding out her hand very politely, limp like Turkish delight, but that was her role.

Jean-Pierre glanced at me, more than a little concerned, and then he shifted the phone to his left hand and held his right out to her.

"Have you got a suitable vehicle?" he asked.

"I'd suggest the Desert Liner, designed for the Paris-Dakar. Eight-wheel drive, three-fifty h.p., cruise control, air conditioning, shower, toilets, kitchen. Neither the dunes nor the wadis nor the snow nor the rocky desert will slow it down, and you'll have all the comforts of home sitting in your armchair in front of the TV."

"That isn't quite what we're looking for," Jean-Pierre said in a pinched voice.

"Twenty thousand francs for six days. It's an unforgettable experience, and it's all on your government's tab. Coffee?"

Jean-Pierre sat cross-legged on the sand, stiff as a rail. He had already had breakfast, thank you anyway, and his travel budget was not expandable. He began asking her questions about geography to test her competence, and suddenly he sounded really well informed; he must have been studying the map all night. His cap blew off his head, and I went after it.

It was warm. Heat rose from the sand; cats and birds were fighting over crumbs. I became distracted for a moment by a kite that was whistling over the ground at the end of its string, held by an immobile little boy in tears who was looking at his sandals. This endless beach where rows of people tanned and read their newspapers, Die Welt, Le Monde, Le Soir, Le Matin, Good Morning, De Morgen, gave off no smell, no sound. No fishermen, no boats, no rocks, no laughter. Behind me, Valerie enthusiastically answered questions with her finger raised, like in school. Watching her, I forgot a bit of my regret over my lost inlet. I brushed off Jean-Pierre's cap, to give myself something to do while they got to know each other.

When I returned, we settled on a Land Rover at nine hundred dirhams for six days, plus gas. Jean-Pierre began to relax. I allowed myself to point out that with his Lorraine skin and no hat, he was going to fry. Valerie snatched up his tube and, without asking, put cream on his forehead, cheeks, and nose. I saw that he threw a few surreptitious glances at her bikini top, and that made me happy. And then his phone rang; he jumped up, scattering sand everywhere, and walked off to take the call. It wasn't Clementine, because I heard "Yes, sir," and suddenly he seemed much less like a little boy. Almost manly, in a tight-assed kind of way. They had given him a responsibility, he was fulfilling it, but they should not reproach him for it or blame the Moroccan national, and they should give him the time and resources to accomplish his mission, he said while kicking into the waves. I liked him like that. I was proud that he was standing up for himself and me. I turned back toward Valerie to make sure she saw it, too, but she was much less impressed.

"That guy's a dink."

"A what?"

"A dink."

I watched Jean-Pierre pacing in the water, his trousers rolled up, socks in his left hand, telephone at his ear. He had hung up with his boss and was trying Clementine's answering machine again, I'd have bet anything: he'd gone back to being a little boy.

"We have to make him fall in love with you," I murmured between clenched teeth.

"Well, let him fall!" she sighed with pure-bred Bordeaux refinement, stretching her upper body. "Put some cream on me?"

She turned over on her stomach and undid her top. I spread the lotion on her back, keeping my eyes on Jean-Pierre, who was sadly listening to the beep from the full answering machine and dragging his feet in the sand.

"I know you think he's weird . . ."

She answered, "No."

"Really?"

"'All the characteristic behavior that we can observe in geese who have lost their partner,'" she continued with a yawn, "'can be found to a large degree in humans suffering pain.'"

Suddenly Jean-Pierre let out a scream, dropped the phone in the water, and ran limping toward us, his arms flailing.

"Konrad Lorenz, *On Aggression*, chapter eleven," Valerie concluded, turning on her side and leaning on one elbow.

Red with pain, wearing a terrible grimace, Jean-Pierre fell onto our breakfast, one leg in the air. He suddenly grabbed Valerie's bikini top and tied it around his calf in a tight tourniquet. And here I was trying to engineer a gentle love story, with campfires in the Atlas and mutual discovery of broken hearts.

"Hey, asshole, you want the bottom too?" Valerie shouted, sending the towel I was trying to cover her breasts with skidding across the sand.

"It's a jellyfish," Jean-Pierre panted. "It happened to me once in Ramatuelle. I'm allergic . . . I've . . . I've got my doctor's number in the room . . ."

Then he slid onto his side on the mat, shaking. The guy really was no travel gift, I'll say that much.

Her cheeks puffy with rage, Valerie jumped to her feet, pulled on her T-shirt, and spat at me, "Now you see why I prefer geese."

She ran toward the narrow path bordering the beach, behind the eucalyptus bushes. I was already writing off our entire trip when she returned with a friendly looking guy who helped me carry the attaché to his taxi.

"It hurts," moaned Jean-Pierre.

"You'll be fine," I said.

The vacationers interrupted their volleyball game as we passed, and I felt ashamed to be lugging this ridiculous clown across the beach in his desert hero costume and a bikini top twisted around his calf. I felt both shame and pain for him.

"We brring you to clinic, Meester," the driver was saying. "They feex you."

And I was angry at the driver, too, for using that lame accent to speak my language. I would gladly have had a go at him, Arab to Arab, just so that for once I could communicate, in a way I understood, that I had had it up to *here*. Instead, I tossed the clown onto the back seat where he stammered in a panic, "What . . . what about my phone?"

"God damn it!" I said.

His teeth began chattering again, and then he fainted, his head on my shoulder, while the stinking 404 jolted us over the sand road. Valerie had it right: the guy really was a dink. She took my hand over the knees of the attaché, whom we volleyed back and forth between our shoulders, and it calmed me down to feel that we were both equally annoyed and that we knew it without saying a word. Something passed between us, I don't know what, something I had never known before, like a meeting between her years of useless studies to end up a guide, and mine wasted breaking into cars, regretting so bitterly having had to leave school. We complemented each other, in a godforsaken way, on either side of this attaché from hell who we felt like shipping back home with a note for his wife. But I've never been able to stay selfish for very long—maybe because I have nothing to defend.

I let go of Valerie's hand. At the same moment, we both tightened our fingers over Jean-Pierre's knees, as he mumbled his nightmares, and her gesture made me fall in love with her even more. When you got down to it, what I wanted was for her to mother this kid for me so that I could feel like a father. Maybe that came from my childhood, I don't know, but it also came from her: I knew we would need something more intelligent than just fucking for us to keep loving each other, she and I.

I stared at her, emotions welling up, and suddenly I realized the attaché was beginning to swell. His allergy was no joke: he was starting to block our view with his edema, and I turned away because despite everything, I suddenly felt like laughing. Valerie must also have been thinking that he was going to keep inflating until he crushed us against the car doors. I could hear little squeaks as she held back her own laughter, and they were like the sweet music of complicity. Maybe I had no right to be happy at such a time, but you never know what sorrows lie in wait, so it's always worth taking a moment of happiness when it comes along: that was my philosophy, and for once I could share it.

The clinic was a new building on a hill, much fancier than the St. Joseph dispensary in North Marseilles. A doctor in a spanking white smock took delivery of the patient on a gurney, then came back to ask us who we were so he could fill out his forms.

"Just a passing friend," I said.

"And you?" he asked Valerie.

"I'm the owner of the bikini top."

He raised his head, remarked that the tourniquet she'd improvised from her bathing suit was much too tight and that the patient had been in danger of gangrene. Valerie added that he was also allergic, though she didn't know to what; in any case, the doctor told her, they had already given him a shot, and they'd have to wait and see. He left without taking his forms.

I whispered to Valerie that I thought he was strange. She answered that at least it wasn't Ramadan: the year before, her father had had his gall-bladder operated on during the fasting season, and the surgeon had fainted while sewing him up. To dispel the bad omen, I asked what her father did in life. She said he was a doctor, as it happened, but he'd quit because of drinking; now he was a gardener. It was out of despair: when his wife had died, the world had ended for him.

I suddenly felt very sad, because I knew that if Jean-Pierre died on his gurney, everyone's world would keep turning all the same. His Clementine would become a widow, which is always more flattering than divorcée, and his parents in the Lorraine would suffer, naturally, but they remembered a young writer of seventeen. They didn't know the pathetic humanitarian attaché with his little suitcase, mobile phone, and baseball cap. That deceased was mine alone, and maybe I would be the only one to mourn the person he really was, but it felt good to cry over someone. At least I'd counted for him, and he left a void in me because he hadn't left me by choice.

Half an hour later they handed him back to us, deflated, trotting along, happy to have triumphed over his allergy, whereas the last time, you won't believe it, I was delirious for three days straight with a temp of 104. He begged our pardon for the inconvenience and insisted on buying Valerie a new bathing suit. I sensed he was beginning to like her, and I waited in the taxi while they went shopping. He seemed a bit disappointed that I wasn't sharing his cheerfulness, but I needed a little time to get over my grief: after all, I'd only just buried him thirty minutes before.

6

Mission diary
Jean-Pierre Schneider
Agadir–Irghiz (Morocco)

Wednesday 25
Clear skies, sunny, 77°.

Departure at 2 p.m. via Route P32, which runs from Agadir to Ouarzazate. We cross the Sous Valley, a lush region where shepherds graze their sheep amid olive trees and argans with long spiny branches, which are the cause of our first stop, due to a flat. Aziz changes the tire.

The shepherds in burnoose run up from all sides to give us a hand, or so I innocently believed—in fact, sadly, their intent was merely to beg. Our guide stops me from opening my wallet, claiming that there are too many of them. As a compensation for these unfortunates, she teaches me my first Arab expression: "Achib Allah," *which means* "Allah will provide." *I say it to them, gradually improving my pronunciation, saving the best for last. I'm joking, but I'm distressed by this poverty that isn't really poverty: more like a reflex. The Westerner is guilty, as always: wherever he goes, he acculturates, creating need. Achib Allah. Delicacy of a ritual grafted onto sordid reality.*

It reminds me of that wonderful sentence by Lucien Guitry when, seeing a blind man sitting against a wall, he gives his son, little Sacha, a gold coin for him to place in the man's hat. "Why didn't you smile at the man when you gave him alms, Sacha?" "But, Father, he's a blind man." *And Lucien Guitry replies,* "Yes, Sacha, but what if he's a false blind man?"

Once Aziz finishes the repairs, we head off again. I'm eager to leave this tourist valley. But I'm also perfectly aware of the initiatory nature of this journey, and every part of it is important.

Tolerable heat. Aziz is sitting in front. I'm in the back seat, above the spare gas cans, and the stream of air flowing through my window has gradually dissipated my car-sickness. Aziz's head is turned toward the snowy peaks of the Atlas that we're beginning to see on the left-hand side. I can imagine the anxiety he's feeling: I will try to translate it into words later, when all is quiet. These are just some notes, a travel

*log attesting to the authenticity of the journey, while help-
ing me avoid the pitfalls of memory a posteriori.*

*I'm jotting down these lines at the edge of a waterfall,
amid tables full of German picnickers running roughshod
over the harmony of the spot. Oleander. Date palms. Prickly
pears. Camels for rent. I saw, on the official map, that the
guide made a thirty-mile detour from our planned itinerary
so we could admire this view. Remember to tell her, tonight
or tomorrow, privately, that we're not here for* sightseeing.
*Any unnecessary local color, no matter how vivid, that does
not explicitly figure on the route Aziz traced out is* irrelevant.

*We fly through Taroudannt and its souks, its bougainvillea,
its 18th-c. ramparts that storks nest in. Miss d'Armeray has
sensed my impatience. Or rather, my rigor. I am not here to*
discover, *but to welcome. I am preparing myself. In training.*

*So many years since I've written. The style. Think about
the style.*

*PS: At the police check in Taliouine, I saw on her pass-
port that her full name is d'Armeray de Villeneuve. I used
to know a Villeneuve in prep school. Ask her if she's related?*

Thursday 26
Same weather.

*Night spent at Club Karam, the luxury hotel in Ouarza-
zate. Despicable. Air conditioning, room service. I demand*

that from now on we sleep at people's houses, or at worst in a country inn. And anyway, hang it all, our equipment includes tents! Let's camp out! The aseptic atmosphere of international hotels has no place in our story.

As for Ouarzazate, no comment. *Foreign Legion barracks turned into a movie set. Busloads of Americans parade by toward the clay village where they claim Orson Welles shot* Sodom and Gomorrah. *Souvenir cigars, "authentic" director's chairs with his name on the back. Pathetic.*

I try to renew contact with Aziz. He avoids me. I don't understand his attitude. He seemed so in tune with my enthusiasm at Rabat airport, when we laid the foundations of our book. I need his eye on his country: he is the narrative instance. My own reactions are unimportant, and I'm doing my best to keep them hidden. But if Aziz's reactions don't take up the slack, there will be nothing left to say and the story will fall apart.

Perhaps Aziz feels inhibited by the presence of the "third party." I should speak to Valerie about it, but that's difficult too. I feel an obstacle hanging between us, and again it's Aziz. He's noticed the attraction she seems to feel for me—while doing an excellent job of pretending not too, incidentally: her instinctive coldness is necessary to the role she occupies, with every male past the age of puberty coming on to her. Could Aziz, with his twenty-year-old physique, his youth, his smile, his shoulders, actually be jealous of me?

If that were true, it would be problematic for our novel, but delicious for me. Thirty-three years old in six months. My God.

*"What have you done with your talent?," yes, I know. But who
am I fighting for? I had forgotten women's glances, since my
wife stopped looking at me. Valerie d'Armeray de Villeneuve.
Never mind.*

PS: *There is nothing sexual in the feelings she shows toward me. It's simply a cultural complicity. Strange that she
should have let herself be abused that way, she, with her
sheltered childhood in Bordeaux, reeking of boarding school,
mass on Sundays, embroidered sheets, piano and golf les-
sons. She identifies with me, she believes I'm defined by the
diplomatic sticker on my suitcase. Maybe she even takes me
for the black sheep of the political-industrial Schneiders from
Creusot, whom the history professors call "Schnèdre" to shine
in front of their students. The benediction of names you don't
pronounce the way they're written: ready-to-wear culture.
Whereas the prince, the heir, the last-of-the-line, the ongoing
tradition is Aziz. I come out of the prole newspaper on Sundays, respecting your boss during the week, life planned in advance, in resignation, from the small house to the factory and
the factory to the café: the brotherhood of workers with its
touching pride in a job well done—everything I broke from.*

*But she too is a rebel. Those fine locks, that hair meant
to be put in a bun that she's massacred with kitchen shears,
that skin with no makeup, the tattoo on her arm, her macho
way of speaking Arabic with her chin jutting forward, those
spitting consonants. Rebellious, insubordinate. She chose
dirt roads, wadis, huge open spaces. I chose books, freedom,*

studies. To end up where? Official delegate temporarily attached to the Press. And she, a dusty ragamuffin among pigheaded tourists who photograph Tuaregs tamed into postcard vendors.

At the restaurant last night, behind those grotesque menus bound like a book of spells, the blue line of her gaze on my hands. My short, thick, idle hands. Made to pour molten metal, for three generations: so inept at holding a pen. And yet—If you could see me, Valerie, at this moment, on my plastic chair, sitting with a yogurt that is soaking up my wheat germ, in the middle of this balcony that looks out on the summits of the High Atlas, writing, writing without seeing any of these wonders that I couldn't care less about. The only thing that counts are these hands that are trying to express who I am. These hands that I've always hidden, in cocktail parties at the Quai, dinners in town. I was proud to offer them to you last night. Let you intuit my renunciation, my flight, in exchange for the regrets lingering around your eyes.

Eight o'clock—time to go.

PPS: I want her.

Friday 27
Puffy clouds, cooler temperatures.

Clementine is drifting away. She's the only one who ever believed in me. She left me when I stopped believing. But

finding my words again won't bring her back; it's too late.
I'm writing without you, Clem. Will you read me? I'll dedi-
cate this novel to you, if I manage to finish it. People say
farewell any way they can.

A touching road sign on the way out of Ouarzazate, a
crudely painted camel indicating to old-style nomads that
Timbuktu is only fifty-two days away by caravan.

First truly untamed landscape: abrupt gorges with red
boulders, where the Land Rover dips into the potholes of a
rocky road bordering a silver wadi. Sublime. I didn't hear
the name, what with the noise of the engine. We have left
Route P32. Finally! Not a single tourist left in sight: the
adventure begins. A few Chleuh Berbers are hitchhiking.
Valerie doesn't stop. Through my open window I call to
them, "Achib Allah!"

A diffuse excitement hangs over the car. The shared feel-
ing of really penetrating into the heart of our quest, of being
on the road to Irghiz for real. And then Aziz's silence, always,
but different now, turned like a favorable wind. As if the
smiles Valerie sends me in the rearview mirror—bright smiles,
of friendship, patient curiosity—as if these smiles are a re-
assurance for him. I was mistaken: he isn't jealous of me
(pretentious!). Sensing my interest in Valerie, he was sim-
ply afraid that a refusal on her part might poison the cli-
mate of our expedition. Now that Valerie has stopped being
defensive, he's relaxing. He's already set himself up as our
go-between. Aziz, my scout, the lighter of my path, is get-
ting his matches ready.

The boy breaks my heart. His simplicity, his delicacy in silence, the benevolent attention he bestows on me, the maturity of a child old as the stones, who has seen the centuries flow around his certainties. He's the one who will give this book its mythic dimension. Everything will be centered on this character in whom I can someday say "I," if I make his point of view, his imagination, my own. For I know perfectly well where we're going. I'm not a fool. His valley of Irghiz is a simple oasis at the foot of a jebel; we've already seen three others like it. His gray men are Chleuh Berbers like any other, whom he deified to get me to love his country—a normal, healthy reaction. I would do the same today if I talked about Uckange, the glorious mythology of the foundry beyond our little garden, where in reality I was bored shitless for seventeen years in the din of the blast furnace and the sirens that drilled through my sleep.

Much more disconcerting is his systematic refusal to speak Arabic. It's Valerie who orders for us at the inn, asks for a fill-up at the mhatta d'lessence *(gas station), shows my official pass at police checks. Why is Aziz on strike against his own tongue? Shame at having his compatriots see him brought back home in a paddy wagon—unmarked, but a paddy wagon all the same? Or else tact toward me, who have to get into his skin despite the language barrier? Unless he speaks a different dialect from the one we're encountering on the road. Something to explore.*

As we were getting gas, I asked the question I've been holding in since Marseilles, so as not to disturb his return

to the source: who had taught him to speak French so well?
Someone from his tribe? Mr. Giraudy? Instead of answer-
ing, he asked me, "What about you?" I didn't understand.

But at noon, in the village of Msinar, during a stop for
lunch that at my request we made at a private citizen's home,
Aziz went even further. He took off his shoes when entering,
like us, to respect the custom, but at the table he committed
an inconceivable, unbelievable act. As there were no uten-
sils, he ate with his fingers, but using his left hand, which is
very serious and constitutes a deliberate offense in the Atlas,
where the left hand is considered impure—as Valerie explained to me when the private citizen threw us out of his
home.

Strange Aziz. Provocative, irreligious, uncultured, igno-
rant of his own traditions? No. He is throwing me a line.
He is causing incidents to spice up my book. It's extraordi-
nary, what's happening to me. I thought he was a muse, and
now I find myself with a kind of "guardian demon" who
tempts and provokes the events and people on his path just
to provide me with material.

I can imagine what our trip would have been like in the
Jeep with that Omar I'd dug up. Not even a chapter: five
pages. Thank you, Aziz. (Chokran, or, more solemnly:
Baraka Allah oufik. *Literally, may Allah grant you bene-*
ficial strength.)

At five o'clock, during a stop in the admirable Jaffar cir-
que (herds of camel, old cedars, juniper trees, the impassable
mass of the snow-covered Ayachi Jebel), taking advantage of

Aziz's absence as he was answering a call of nature in the broom shrubs, I questioned Valerie about the myth of Irghiz. She half-heartedly confirmed his version of the "sacred valley" where prehistoric plants and animals still survived, but surprisingly in an almost reproachful tone, as if debating an offensive skepticism on my part (is skepticism the moral "left hand" in the Atlas?).

In a word, it felt like I was talking UFOs with a specialist from NASA who reeled me off the standard info: speed statistics, radar echoes, traces of matter. Analytic rigor in the service of a conceivable hypothesis. (NB: reinsert my impressions of the "Frontiers of Science" conference in Puy-Saint-Vincent, where the director of Books and Literature had me accompany that Spanish physicist who claimed he was receiving formulas of an important molecular discovery—authenticated—from the extraterrestrial Umnite civilization. A KGB plot to discredit European scientists, according to Loupiac. I have always opposed this version. Tell why. No to the systematic refusal of dreams. Respect what is beyond us.)

So, Valerie showered me with paleontological references: the imprints of saurian fossils from Imi-n-Ifri (25 million years old) and their large eggs found in a state of supernatural preservation, the locations of the Neolithic cults of Tizi n'Tirghist, the thousands of rupestrine engravings from Tinsouline and Draa, entirely executed with a burin (10,000 years old). According to her, Morocco abounded in miraculous vestiges, unspoiled places, indecipherable secrets. There were hundreds of Irghizes hidden in the unattainable pockets *of the High Atlas. And the paved road under construction that threatened the valley of the gray men was the CT1808, being built to serve a future ski resort on the Ouaoulzat Jebel (12,500 feet up), a shameful gash-in-progress that we'd driven by not long before.*

When Aziz returned, she asked him to back her up, and he did. She asked if it was still far. He planted himself in the middle of the cirque, hands on his back, and turned slowly, seeming to search the blinding white of the summits for the least difficult pass to cross. She said something to him in Arabic, which he answered with a long, very serious nod. Then she looked at me. She didn't want to translate what she had said.

Succulent meal this evening in a tighremt, *a kind of ochre-colored fortified house with windows lined in white to repel evil spirits* (jnoun). Mint tea, harira (*unidentified soup*), tajine *with prunes,* kefta (*meat balls*), *huge chilies that I ate, mistaking them for sweet peppers, and two liters of water to put out the fire, despite Valerie's warning about bacteria. I didn't care. As far as I'm concerned, the only impurity to avoid now is my left hand. Thirty-two years of Evian water—enough. I want to live. I've thrown out my wheat germ.*

In the terra cotta village where I'd gone to sweat out of their sight, my throat on fire, among the goats and durmast oaks, Valerie came to join me. We sat on the tires. She took my hand. As if by magic, the sweat soaking my polo shirt seemed to stop dripping. She admitted to me that Aziz couldn't find the path to his valley. I said we had time. That I had a terrible desire to have time, for once in my life. She put her lips on mine, kissed me for nearly twenty seconds. When she pulled away, her chin raised, eyes barred by a stray lock, she asked me if that was better. I answered yes. She murmured that she had blocked the effect of the chili peppers, and there was no point in jumping her.

I watched her walk away toward the casbah. Her slim and desperately young silhouette, living, inaccessible. How can you propose love to a fairy who is making fun of you? Has she ever even made love? There's something utterly virginal about her: a harsh freedom, a dreamy intransigence, an elusive melancholy. Perhaps that's what she's trying to tell me. I've never deflowered anyone. Agnes, Agnes—How far away you are, in my room in Uckange, when I read you my manuscript and, sitting amid the notebooks, intoxicated by the sentences you had just heard, you, my only reader, I kissed you on the bed, fondled you, and you said no, you said "read some more." So I read.

If we are meant to make love, Valerie, and if it's your first time, I believe I'll be as much a virgin as you. Suddenly I'm fifteen years old. And by the way, your kiss did not lessen the effect of the chilies in the slightest.

I am happy. Right?
We'll see.

First night under the stars. I ripped the yellow tent by accident while trying to cut a cord that was too long. Valerie sets up the green one and moves in. Immediately she turns off the gas lamp.

At one in the morning, terrible storm, of Dantesque violence. Aziz and I, soaked, take refuge in the Land Rover. Ten minutes later, a torrent of mud comes out of nowhere and washes away the tent we'd just vacated. We run to knock on Valerie's tent, open the zipper. Half asleep, she curses at us, tells us to "piss off." The torrent flows three yards from her slumber. We hesitate to pull her out by force, and then we go to stand watch from behind the windshield, keeping an eye on the flood until the end of the storm.

It's seven in the morning. The temperature has dropped fifteen degrees. Valerie has just come out of her tent, wrapped in a sweater. I turn on the headlights so she can see where she's walking, climb out to bring her the thermos. She casts a distracted glance at the edge of last night's flood, and says something to me that I'll remember for the rest of my life: "People who no longer love life know perfectly well when they're going to die. I was in no danger."

She goes to pee behind her tent, then crawls back in to sleep. Dawn begins to show, the sky is limpid again, turns blue under the stars. I screw the cap back on the thermos and get into the car to write, using the steering wheel for support. Aziz, huddled in his quilt against the door, grumbles for me to turn off the overhead light, because of the battery. He falls back asleep. High up in the sky, an eagle circles around us.

I reread the sentence Valerie said. It will be the epigraph to my book. My book. I don't know any longer what will be in it. I couldn't care less about Irghiz, the gray men, the Quai d'Orsay, my mission, the reintegration of Aziz, who is reintegrating all by himself. Valerie, Valerie, Valerie. Sigh.
I lay down my pen to finish my sentence in a dream.

Sunday 29
Radiant sun, 70°.

I don't know where to start. My life is tipping over.
I didn't record the day, last night. Wasn't able to.
Marvelous, harrowing, inexpressible.
What good are adjectives?
Saturday morning, at ten to eight, Valerie came to pound on my door. I woke up, opened it. She yanked me from the Land Rover and dragged me to the edge of a sheer drop. Before my eyes, the desert was flowering. The colors mauve, yellow, red, and blue surged up one by one from the bare soil. As I hugged her against me, transported by enthusiasm, she answered that she had nothing to do with it: it's a natural phenomenon. Rare, but natural. Like love. The seeds of the Atlas can wait for years for enough rain to let them bloom, and then they explode into life, all at once, at the first ray of sunlight.
I lay my head on her shoulder. She puts her arm around my waist. A moment of plenitude, absolute, certainty—I'll work out the sentences later. Words refuse to come; I fear

*banality almost as much as lyricism. I would like to write to
her and wait for a reply, but I've wasted too many moments
in my life. So I take her by the hand, run to the small lake
near our camp and dive into the water with her, among the
startled pink flamingos, wrap my arms around her in the
waves and let us fall over. She cries out, "No, not here, careful!" and repeats a name I don't recognize, Bill something,
another man she loves or who drowned here, what does it
matter?*[3] *Nothing exists now but her body in our splashes of
water. The world is ours, deserted apart from Aziz who is
heating up the coffee somewhere over there. I throw her down
in the silt, undress as if I were handsome, she sighs and, on
this bed that sinks beneath us, she offers herself to me.*

*Description later: I'm still in shock. I was clumsy, brutal,
I know it, but I wanted her too much, needed her too much,
and she let me come into her with resignation. When I realized I'd been the only one to climax, I said to her, feeling
contrite, sheepish, "Achib Allah," as if to a beggar you haven't
given anything to. She was kind enough to smile. I love you.
You answered, "Oh, come on." You'll see, when I've written
a book about it.*

*Helping you get up, I asked you, in a state of doubt (but
if one is going to appear ridiculous, might as well seem
naïve), if I was the first. You replied, aggressively, but perhaps out of modesty or pride, "In the water, yes!"*

---

[3] In fact, bilharziosis, an intestinal illness caused by a trematode worm
that sea mollusks transmit to humans. She explained it to me later.

We walked out of the lake and the flamingos returned behind our backs. Without looking back, you dove into your tent. I went to see Aziz who had gone off to sit on a rock, on the edge of the wadi where he was trying to skip stones. He had seen us, of course. He was crying. Standing next to him, shading him from the sun, I offered my apologies. He answered that he wasn't crying because of us, but because of the water. Because of lovemaking in the water. When I tried to find out more, he began talking about an immense underground clearing, the bottom of an ancient dead volcano where plane trees and umbrella pines grew thanks to the light falling through the crater. Miniature horses of a forgotten race cantered around the warm springs in which Lila bathed while singing amid the water lilies, Lila, his beloved, the daughter of the king of Irghiz who would never give her to a simple lark (sic), and that was why he had volunteered to go find Mr. Giraudy in Marseilles, and why he was in such despair today to be coming back empty-handed — he didn't blame me, he explained — but it was no coincidence that the entrance to the valley was evading him: his left hand, having been seen by men, had become impure.

I'm jotting down the broad lines, from memory; the vision of this handsome boy infused with sunlight, crying over the image of some imaginary volcano, left me cold. I no longer want his story, all of a sudden. My own is beginning. He can keep us turning in circles around his mountain for weeks; I'm in love and I have time on my side.

Is it true, then, that one can become selfish so quickly when one is happy? I looked at my watch. I wanted to remember that at nine-forty-four on this Saturday morning, I forgave Clementine.

And what was I forgiving her for? For having liked Lorraine, my manuscript that I read to her one afternoon at the university dining hall; for having held publisher dinners at her mother's house where over dessert I was asked to read several pages as an "appetizer"? Ridicule is what killed us. Or me, at least. She's rich. And it's easier with a painter. Ten seconds are all you need to get an idea, just by looking at the wall; a painter is much less intrusive than a writer. And the truth is, Loupiac's paintings aren't bad.

Before lunch, romantic walk on my own, thinking of Her, my new Her, Valerie d'Armeray de Villeneuve, my sweetness, my siren, all along the wadi. Stomach cramps. I think they're psychosomatic.

Aziz brings mules for us to try to climb the south face: the passage is up there, he remembers, he confirms. I let him go. Gastric troubles.

Valerie attends to her business, draws lines on the maps, manipulates her compass to make up for the incompetence of our gray man. She doesn't seem put off by my little problems. "I know all about illness," she told me. On the other hand, she warned me that tenderness, vows, the future, everything I'm burning to offer her, she refuses. As for making love again, she tells me first to take the medicines she's picked out for me from her pharmaceuticals case. I'm a bit con-

---

cerned to see they've all expired. She lays a hand on my forehead, grips my wrist, and answers that it's them or me. I hope she's joking.

She has diagnosed a bacterial infection. The water in which we knew each other? No, the water I drank last night. So much the better.

Aziz comes back early in the evening, on muleback. He tells us that the access must be on the north face. Seeing me shivering under my quilt, he asks Valerie what's wrong with me now. She answers in Arabic. He turns away, sighing. They won't translate for me.

Monday
Gray skies, 101°.

Refused to go see a doctor in Tabant. Too bad for the fever: it will go down, and we'll cross the pass. Never again will I turn back. The novel will be called One-Way.

My stomach is knotted up in cramps, and I have a strange kind of vertigo, not unpleasant. It takes me somewhere else. I am getting close to something, in my head. Something essential that eludes me under the effect of the aspirin, but I'll get it back.

Too tired to write down my dreams. Scattered words, hoping they'll recall images: Henri IV—Lebanon—croissants—water lilies—cake.

My foot has begun swelling again where the jellyfish infected it, and Aziz has to help me walk when we break camp. We still circle around the mountain chain: he can't find the entrance. Not a problem. Better. Time.

Wait for night, with Her, in the tent. Rediscover my room, Agnes, the words coming out of my notebook for her. Agnes married, with children, asked to be the godfather. Refused, why? So much pain. All those years wasted, ruined. For what? Shame. Shame for what I did. The platform of Gare de l'Est. No. No words. Not yet. Forget.

Wednesday?

Wind, sun. My fever has gone down. I stay in the tent while they explore. The weekend in Bruyères. The little house with the faded trompe-l'oeil that Dad restored during vacations, with the foundry team. Vacations taken in turns, the shared walls showing traces of each man's taste: the house changing—Summer in the Vosges. My first weekend with Agnes, first time she's said yes. Alone with her. And Dad. You're a minor, Jean-Pierre, I'm coming with you. He slept in the Simca, beneath our window. For Mom. She'd entrusted him with the mission, but he left us our night. Our night during which we did nothing. I love you, Dad. I never said it, I wrote it, though I didn't dare let you read it. Tadeee! Tadaaa! Taratata! at eight in the morning, to warn us, so we'd have time to get decent: he was bringing up croissants. I wasn't ashamed of you, Dad, I swear it. In your work overalls, with your checkered cap and your meaty face covered in plaster: you had been building a partition in the basement for the past two hours. "So how are the lovebirds this morning? Been behaving yourselves?" A riot. No, no shame at him this time. Only shame at myself. And hatred of Agnes, who had refused me her body and now refused my father, her strained face turned to the wall, sheets squeezed under her arms to hide her not-even-naked chest. My only weekend with a girl. Before Clem. Never again did I have morning croissants with bits of plaster in them. I did resent you for that, Dad—I resented you so much. It was so easy to accuse you. You didn't even know that you were in my book. That it was about your life. And you would no longer exist for me except on paper. To deny that you drank, that you were getting old, that you played the trumpet and snored at the table. Life burned out by the blast furnace you worshipped, your pride and joy. Forgive me, Dad. Forgive me for afterward. Forgive me for the station. It hurts.

One evening

My fever has returned. Valerie taking care of me. I won't read this over. I want it to come out. Day of shame. Double shame.

I'd just been appointed to Quai d'Orsay. Telex dept. Bureaucrat. Diplomat. I had something to show them,

FINALLY, I was somebody, I hadn't left for nothing. I sent them train tickets. We'd celebrate. At the Hunter's Clarion, Dad's restaurant, his only memory of Paris, his night in the capital, in '39. Before leaving for the front. Came by train, left by train, prisoner for four years, then the train back, 79 pounds. And I waited for them at the station. To reconcile. This time it was a joyful train. My son has made it.

Traffic jams, accident, insurance information, I got there half an hour late. When I saw them, the two of them, ruddy-complexioned, fat, in their Sunday best, plaid jacket, the neighbor's fur coat borrowed once before for my brother's wedding, I couldn't do it. The yellow leatherette suitcase, the plastic shopping bag with the cake. Her cake. Impossible to move, to take a single step toward them, to force myself, face up to their anger, ask their forgiveness. Forgiveness for being late, for being alive, for wanting to do something else, for not staying in touch, for loving a Paris girl. They shouted at each other, argued, appealed to the train conductor who shrugged his shoulders. I couldn't move. Couldn't breathe. I saw myself in the café window, the three-piece suit, round glasses. Me? That office thing, that uniform, that dead dream, that figure out of a Magritte painting? Me, the writer, the Romantic lover, the poet of Lorraine who had dedicated his manuscript to the singer Bernard Lavilliers, another one who came from the foundry, our hero, our rebel, with his memory at war and his rebellion expressed in an earring? Is this what I had become? A hanger wearing a suit.

I didn't move, didn't call out. I stood there as they finally headed to another platform to take the train home. Dad was yelling. Mom in tears. The cake fallen out of the bag. I didn't move. The double shame. Shame of what they still were, shame of what I had become so as not to be like them.

When the train to Metz departed with its red taillights, I went over to pick up the cake. I kept it, not daring to eat it. It's still at Boulevard Malesherbes, in my closet. Clem must have thrown it out by now.

My hand is too unsteady. I've said it all. I won't know how to love them until after they're dead. And what if I died first? I called Uckange later that evening. Sorry, I'm in Lebanon, urgent mission, couldn't get word to you on time, sent my secretary but he missed you, really sorry, I'll come out there at Christmas. Enough, Jean-Pierre. Your father knows perfectly well that you're ashamed of us. You didn't have to do that to him. Just leave us alone, it's the best thing for all concerned, go live your life. My life.

Please, let me be read.

7

It's now been three days since he stopped writing in his notebook. His right foot has started swelling again, where the jellyfish stung him, and he can no longer tie his shoe. He's often sick because of his allergies and the spices he insists on eating to be like the locals. His face is one big sunburn that manages to stay pale at the same time. He must have lost ten pounds. But maybe it's from love.

I've taken to sleeping in the Land Rover at night, to leave them the tent. Valerie says nothing about what goes on between them, and I turn away when her storm lamp starts casting their shadows on the canvas. In any case, we barely talk anymore. We look, we drive, we make camp. And I remain alone with the bright red sunrises over the stone deserts, and orange sunsets on the snowy peaks, my feet on the dashboard, in the emptiest silence I've ever known, broken twice a day by the huffing of a turbo: the Desert Liner passing below, cutting trails at sixty miles an hour to transport its cargo of pampered explorers.

One morning, beside a waterfall over black rocks, I was watching the sun rise as usual, comparing it with the one from the day before, when I saw Valerie emerge from the tent in my rearview. She walked up to the waterfall, wrapped in a shawl with long fringes, barefoot in the sub-freezing temperatures. It wasn't an act of bravado, but of indifference. The cold stones had no more effect on her than a man's body. She went to drink some water, stretched, looked at the mountains, shrugged her shoulders, and headed back. Seeing that I was awake behind the windshield, she detoured over. She opened the door, which creaked, put a finger to her lips as if to silence the noise. I had a strong desire to talk to her, even just to say good morning. Looking at me, she let out a sigh, her head to one side, as if wondering what the hell I was doing here, and why she'd agreed to this, and if our presence was really necessary to the sunrise.

"Those colors are beautiful," I said, because the look she was giving me was too painful.

She finished unbuttoning my pants that I'd loosened for the night and rubbed her cheek against me with a tenderness I'd never seen in her, as if she were seeking some sort of kindness before falling asleep. And then she caressed me with her mouth, slowly, while the sun finished rising from its mountain to trace circles on the windshield. It was like hope before the end of the world, the start of something that didn't yet realize it could serve no purpose, the birth of a happiness that ended almost before it began. She swallowed me without a glance, closed the door behind her, and went into the tent. Maybe she was just regaining her strength before going back to play at love for Jean-Pierre. I was no longer sure I wanted what I had chosen, but it was too late to turn back.

Every morning, Valerie drew up a route that led us farther away from civilization, the only way to get closer to Irghiz. The more we climbed through the upper passes only to head down again, ten times a day, the more our lives seemed to grow more constricted in that car. The three of us were squeezed into the front, under blankets because the heater had stopped working since Jean-Pierre tried to adjust it. Hood open, monkey wrench in hand, screwdriver between his teeth, he told us that at the age of twelve he knew how to dismantle carburetors in the Lorraine. And then he coughed, and while he was hacking up his lungs we had to look for the screwdriver that had fallen into the engine.

He talked more and more about the Lorraine, as if the fact of having burned his bridges with his wife and his Paris existence brought him back to his childhood, his point of departure. Skirting the sheer drops, crossing the wadis, bumping over trails in search of nothing, we heard the sound of the blast furnaces, the whistle, the sirens, the molten metal pouring into the well, and the friendships between men at three thousand degrees. That entire unknown world that began on the other side of the garden wall.

The small house squeezed among others that were the same, with all the alarm clocks set to the same time, the same future, the same school, the same unemployment. And the Smurfs who waited patiently for the factory to shut down, the people to leave, and life to disappear so they could take over the site. Jean-Pierre said the French government had sold the death of the Lorraine to Germany so that the Ruhr would live. I no longer knew what dream we were in, if we were heading toward an imaginary valley or a foundry from the past. Valerie drove, indifferent, pilot during the day, mistress at night, certain of her route that led nowhere.

And then we hit a breakdown. At 6,300 feet, in a wind that blew half sand, half snow, we tried for three hours to repair, but all the parts we removed immediately became covered in sand and we didn't know what we were doing. Jean-Pierre had forgotten, the only car parts I knew about were radios, and Valerie sent CB calls into the void. We tried to set up the tent, but it blew away. Our food supplies were intact, but the can opener had disappeared. We seemed to have a curse against us, which Jean-Pierre, with his bronchitis and his fever and his infected foot, considered a good omen: we were getting close to Irghiz. He could hear the hammering of the forge, and the gray men had unleashed the elements to signal us. I thought he was going insane, but it was worse than that: he was reverting to childhood. He called Valerie "Agnes," and she seemed to know why; she didn't correct him. We lay him down in the back under all the blankets we had. When he went to join his dreams in sleep, she told me it was finished: she was stopping the game. As soon as the storm blew over, we would head down to Bou-Guemes, where the Desert Liner came through twice a day. I said no: we couldn't go back without finding Irghiz. She cried out that I was nuts, that Jean-Pierre was sick and we had to send him home as a medical emergency. I answered that nothing was waiting for him back there, that his life was playing itself out here, and that we should play it out for him to the end, by show-ing him Irghiz so he could finish his book. She didn't say anything more. I wrapped myself up in my jacket against the door and waited for the snow storm to turn into night.

In the morning the sky was clear, and Valerie was gone. I walked along the edge of the cliff, letting pieces of ice crumble off to be lost in the valley below, from which the sharp whistle of the Desert Liner rose for a moment be-fore stopping, then starting up again, no doubt taking our guide with it. She had given us what we'd asked; there was nothing more she could do for us. It was better that way.

When I turned around, Jean-Pierre was walking straight ahead, sinking into the snow where his infected foot didn't seem to bother him anymore. I went to join him. His eyes, shining with fever, didn't even see me. He pointed his finger:

"There it is."

I said yes.

He walked toward a crevasse, smiling. He stumbled a few yards from the edge and couldn't get back up. I helped him. His entire body was trembling, but as if from happiness.

"And yet it's Sunday."

"Yes."

"Seven days a week, Aziz. Eight castings a day: the purest cast iron in the world. So pure that people would process it into dozens of different grades. They make me laugh with their electrical dies . . . I'll tell you this much: no metal heated in electric ovens will ever replace our cast iron. Come with me."

I put his arm across my shoulders and supported him to the entrance of his foundry, where I saw, far in the distance, in a ray of light, the underground pines and plane trees of Irghiz, and the prehistoric horses around a spring where a woman was singing.

"Can you hear it, Jean-Pierre?"

"Yes."

We didn't see the same woman, but it was the same song. The cold of the snow and the blinding sun united us at the edge of the crevasse.

"It's beautiful," I said.

"Yes, it is. I never should have left."

"You did the right thing—you could never have come back otherwise."

He thanked me and slid gently into the snow, with a smile that then stopped.

I carried him to the car. I took the black notebook in his pocket, now all wet, and set it to dry for a moment on the hood. From his suitcase I took his papers, the beginning of the novel he'd written in my file, as well as a large spiral-bound notebook marked *Lorraine*, containing a hundred pages of his childish handwriting. I squeezed all of it under my belt, between my undershirt and my shirt. And then I bashed open a can of tuna with a rock, ate the tuna and drank the oil to give myself energy, hoisted onto my shoulders the small corpse that now weighed only on my heart, and headed back down the trail.

I stopped every ten minutes, to talk to him, because I could tell he was there around me, his soul or his memories, I don't quite know how to say it, but I could feel his presence. It was the warmth of a friendship that told me to go on, you're right, you did the right thing, keep moving; it was an allergy to life that slowly detached me from my body to restore me to my dreams. Keep moving, Aziz. Go all the way to the end, finish my story. I'll guide you. You were right: I was a passing friend.

Two hours later, a huge old American station wagon came to meet us. Valerie flew out of it, screaming, "Now do you see!"

I didn't put up an argument. Her father opened one eye and got out to help us. He was a kind of flabby mountain in a light blue sweatsuit zipped all the way up. His flesh collapsed down a face that was as craggy as the Atlas, with snowy eyebrows and furrowed valleys. His hands shook from alcohol and his forward-leaning head seemed to be pulling his legs along. His voice was deep, steady but gloomy.

"Careful of the dahlias."

We pushed aside the flowerpots, in this ambulance transformed into a greenhouse, to hide the stiffening body of my attaché under some kind of ivy leaves. Her father leaned on my shoulder to close the hatch. He said in a blasé tone, "I'll handle this. I can drop you off in Tabant: the bus for Ouarzazate comes between two and four. Nobody saw you, they'll never find the body, there won't be an investigation for weeks. Do you have any money?"

I answered that I still had fifteen thousand francs from our travel allowance, and that I wasn't about to abandon my attaché.

"Listen to me, kid, disappear into the woodwork and make yourself scarce, okay?"

"Do what Daddy says," Valerie mumbled.

I looked through the back window at my friend's feet, around which ivy twisted: life went on. I said, "I want to bring him back home."

They looked at each other. Valerie seemed bothered, but not surprised. Her father's fist came down on the hood with a metallic bang.

"Get the hell out of here!"

His shout made him lose his balance; he grabbed onto the radio antenna, which started to bend while a string of spit drooled from his lips. With an antiquarian's care, Valerie made him sit down by bending his knees, a cautious hand slipped between his skull and the roof of the car. He let himself be settled in, immediately calmer, with a smile that made his eyes disappear.

Valerie closed the door and spun back toward me. Before I had a chance to open my mouth, she spat fiercely, "He's a wonderful man. He's done some fantastic things here, and I forbid you to judge him. You never know what you're going to become. And it's not his fault."

I said that I knew. She slipped under my arm and led me farther away. She was crying. I wanted to talk to her some more, listen to her, bring her to France with us, but I could tell it was impossible.

"What have we done, Aziz . . . what have we done . . .?"

I murmured that she hadn't done anything, and that she was under no obligation to help me.

"And how will you manage, all by yourself in the middle of the Atlas?"

I let the silence answer for me.

"Are you going back to Marseilles?"

"No. I want to take him back to Paris."

She said all right. The wind lifted her stiff hair, her sand-covered sunglasses fell onto her nose, and I would have liked her to feel grief for Jean-Pierre, or be in love with me—they were the same thing.

"He was in love with you, you know," I said.

"I know. By another name, but so it goes."

"Agnes?"

"Mmhmm."

"Did he ever talk to you about Clementine?"

"Yes, at the beginning. A little. And then not at all."

"Did you feel pleasure with him?"

"That's none of your business."

It was a good answer. It sounded like a yes.

She asked, "So who's Agnes?"

I said it was none of *her* business, so as not to admit I had no idea. Between us, we were Jean-Pierre's memory, and everything we hid from each other was a way of holding onto him a little longer, enriching him. She asked if he was Catholic or something, so she could say a few prayers. I mused aloud that one day, she and I would find each other again and make love, that this would be our prayer. She didn't answer, and we held our hands out to each other, which we kept tightly clasped all the way back to the car.

"Should I call Europ Assistance?" said her father, who had rolled down the car window.

He was holding a thermos that he'd just drunk from, and was breathing easier. I mentioned that I had an official pass from the king.

"Let me see."

I handed him the documents from my humanitarian expulsion. He rolled his window back up to study them. Valerie thanked me. She said he still needed to feel useful, to return sometimes to his world from before. I didn't ask any questions. Where people come from and what they are isn't my problem, unless they feel like talking about it.

Valerie and her father were another story in which I had
no place, where I was of no use.

When he opened his door, I told him I was grateful for
his help. He ordered me to get in and shut up, adding that
no one would ever steal his daughter from him. In a sense
it was true, and I didn't respond to the sorrowful look that
Valerie turned toward me, to see if I had understood what
lay behind his words. She at the wheel, her father next to
her, a flaccid boulder jostled by the potholes in the trail,
and me in back, passenger among the flowers, holding onto
my friend's legs at every jolt—it was a peculiar image of
life. An insane hope grew in me as my fingers tightened
on his cold sock. My hope was that Valerie had gotten
pregnant by Jean-Pierre, and that the two of them, there
in front, would raise the orphan in the image of that amazing father who had discovered the valley of the gray men.
Valerie caught my eye in the rearview mirror and smiled,
without knowing, but I trusted her.

In Marrakech, we went into an administrative building
where Dr. d'Armeray filled out the death certificate and a
stack of forms in Arabic. In the office for the formalities, I
saw Valerie watching him with pride, and I was proud too.
With a steady step and his chin thrust forward, he came
over to hand me the papers and declared, "Heart attack."

I said thanks. He brushed aside my gratitude with a familiar gesture, and with the other hand took from me the
envelope marked "French Republic," which contained our
travel funds.

"Diplomatic pouch?" he suggested.

I didn't know what he meant, but Valerie answered for me that it wasn't necessary. With a disappointed shrug of his shoulders, he went back to disrupting the functionaries who seemed to keep a low profile around him. He must have been important once upon a time, or rich. Part of the mission allowance went to pay for a lead-lined coffin and the requisite stamps. Then we left without Jean-Pierre, who would be brought to the airport as official luggage by the appropriate department, as per the stamped document I had been given. It listed me as Aziz Kamal, special courier from the French consulate. It would make things go faster at customs, the doctor explained. He had misspelled my name, but I couldn't see how that would matter to anyone.

In the parking lot, Dr. d'Armeray, who had been perked up by writing all those forms, did a strange thing: he opened the hatch of the station wagon and threw all his pots of flowers into the courtyard, where they shattered into a mass of drooping leaves.

"Ten years less," he said to me, closing the hatch.

And he hugged his daughter very tightly against him, as she thanked me with her eyes.

We parted at the passport check, she and I. Her father had stayed behind in the car. We searched for words of farewell, stood there looking stupidly at each other in the middle of the scurrying crowd, holding hands to delay the moment, or to make up for lost time. Everything we hadn't said to each other flashed through our eyes, every misunderstanding, every regret, every joy, the essential things and the minor ones. And then, when it was really time for me to board, she asked simply, "Was Irghiz beautiful?"

I murmured, "It was."

And our lives started up again with a promise of nothing, perhaps, but with the happiness of knowing we hadn't spoiled our farewell. We knew we would preserve each other intact, sheltered in our final second when we had fully understood each other, and it was good.

I walked into the plane in a haze of tears that went with the coffin.

8

At Orly-Sud airport, the employee in charge of repatriations asked what extension he should call at Quai d'Orsay. I answered that the party had been notified and was on his way. The employee said fine, pointed me toward the parking lot used in such cases. I said goodbye and went to the men's room, as a transition. When I came out, he was gone. I called information, who gave me the number for a moving company. A truck arrived an hour later, and the movers spat out their chewing gum to load the coffin.

"One-seventeen Boulevard Malesherbes," I said.

I climbed into the cabin with them and we drove in silence, apart from their condolences and my thanks. I found Paris ugly and sad, but it was raining, traffic was slow, and my eyes were still focused on the Atlas, so I couldn't really judge. And then I wrote, leaning on my knees, pages of explanation that I tore up one after the other. I remembered Jean-Pierre crossing out the words of his letter in the airplane. Clearly, Clementine wasn't a woman you wrote to easily. Unable to find anything to say, I decided to talk to her face to face.

The building was old, with an elevator that was too small to fit Jean-Pierre. The movers made him take the stairway, while I went up ahead to the fourth floor. I rang the bell. Fashionable chime, double door, thick carpet, and sconces on the wall. The calling card slipped into the gold-plated frame read, "Clementine Maurais-Schnei." By pushing the card a little to the right, you could erase Jean-Pierre's name completely.

After a moment someone came to answer the door, and it was a man. In a bathrobe, looking intruded upon. That was something I hadn't foreseen. I stammered that I was a friend of Mr. Schneider's. He looked at me as if I were a scratch on his car, then turned around to call, "Titine!" Mrs. Schneider arrived in a dressing gown of beige silk, eyes puffy, face tense. The man: short hair, square jaw, hands on hips. His removable Sony car CD player was lying at the foot of the coat rack, from which his raincoat hung.

She asked, "What is it?"

I looked at this couple, and my mind was made up in three seconds. I told Clementine it was my mistake. I turned back toward the stairs. At the third floor, I asked the movers to turn around, and we brought Jean-Pierre back down.

When the doors to the truck were closed again, I asked them for a map of France. Luckily, Uckange did exist, and I found it right away: it was a small name in the East, next to Thionville which was marked in bold. Out of breath, not pleased, they said their delivery area didn't extend beyond greater Paris. So I took out my Republic envelope, settled the bill, and had them drop me at the Bineau garage, where, as per the ad that I'd just circled in the newspaper folded on the dashboard, a 1980 Citroën C35 van absorbed the last of my mission funds.

9

The window looks out on an apple tree that is losing its final traces of soot to the wind. Everything in his room has remained "as is": the ink-stained coverlet, the little toy cars in a row, the virgin notebooks on the bookshelf, and, on the schoolboy desk of varnished pine, the framed photo of Agnes, the adolescent brunette with a mysterious smile who has become the unhappy blonde I saw the other morning, between her three children and her husband, unemployed like all the men here since the foundry shut down.

His parents greeted me a bit coldly at first, but things got better once I told my story. I had left my Citroën in the parking lot of the Conforama furniture store so that I could introduce myself to them empty-handed, out of politeness. When I tapped at the glazed kitchen door in the back of the blocky little house, with its dirty red roof plunged into shadow by the smokestacks of the cold blast furnace, his mother was ironing and his father drinking coffee, sitting at the table before an open newspaper, cheek on his fist, staring at the wall. I recognized them. A bit older, a bit ruddier, a bit sadder, but they hadn't really changed since Gare de l'Est, since the last page of Jean-Pierre's notebook.

I said I had come because of their son. His mother immediately panicked: "Oh my God, something's happened to Gerard!" Gerard was his brother, the one who stayed— or actually, who moved twenty miles away, to another foundry that wasn't scheduled to close quite so soon. I reassured them the best I could: no, no, Gerard was fine; I'd come on behalf of the *other* one. Jean-Pierre. A glacial silence fell over the room. His mother's mouth dropped open; she looked over at his father, then resumed her ironing. His father turned the page of his newspaper and started to read.

After a while, as I was still standing there, he slowly declared, "There is no more Jean-Pierre."

Clearly, he was handing me the perfect segue. But I couldn't. I saw my Citroën in the Conforama parking lot, with my friend waiting inside. Waiting for what? A reunion? A hole in the ground. All at once, the aim of my trip struck me as ludicrous, idiotic, petty. Bringing them a dead body in place of a living man whom they'd erased from their lives. This wasn't the prodigal son's return. I had the wrong legend.

In one burst, I told the Schneiders that Jean-Pierre was being held captive by a band of Moroccan rebels in

Irghiz, where the French government had sent him with orders to bring me back there. I'd been let go after the ambush, as a non-valuable hostage, and my humanitarian attaché had managed to slip me his manuscripts, along with a message for his parents. The message was, "Please forgive me for the station and for everything. I love you both."

An earthquake shook the kitchen. They ran to the windows, to the phone, rallied the neighbors, the family, their buddies from the foundry; they alerted City Hall, the local officials, the town newspaper. I felt a bit overwhelmed by what I had unleashed, but their son's captivity had revived them in a matter of seconds. They talked about signing petitions, notifying their representative, going as a group to see the superintendent in Metz.

In the tumult of people rushing into the house to get details of the kidnapping, I slipped away. As far as I was concerned, this was just a temporary story: I had only wanted to reconcile the Schneiders with their son before letting him die a hero's death, so they would mourn him as he deserved. I figured I'd wait fifteen minutes, then go tell them the official version, with my deepest apologies and the coffin in the van and, once the shock passed, they'd appreciate my tact. In fact, only the ending was changing. Now that everyone was being mobilized, Jean-Pierre might even be buried with local honors.

Twenty times, in every direction, I walked over the Conforama parking lot. My Citroën C35 was gone. After forty minutes, I decided it was a sign from fate: I stopped looking, stopped asking the passers-by who hadn't seen anything, the towing service that didn't answer, and let matters take their course. I told myself that my distress was nothing compared to what the car thief would feel when he opened the rear door to examine his loot.

For some time afterward, I read the human interest stories every morning in the *Républicain Lorrain*. I never came across a single mention of my van or its cargo. And strange as it seems, at no point did I feel guilty. On the contrary, reality had in a sense made my fiction come true.

I left on foot in the dark small town, among the shuttered houses, the protest posters unglued by rain, and the buildings without balconies on which signs proclaiming "Immediate Occupancy," "For Sale," "For Rent" slapped in the wind. The echo sent me back the sound of my steps in the deserted streets. I was alone in the middle of a ghost town that asked only to be rescued from oblivion; I had crossed half the width of France, guided by the sentiment of my mission. I had no right to leave like this—and where was I leaving for? I had to follow my story to the very end.

As I still had five francs, I called the Ministry of Foreign Affairs. Adopting an Arab accent, I asked for Loupiac's office. I told his secretary I was claiming credit for the kidnapping of Jean-Pierre Schneider, on behalf of an anonymous faction against the CT 1808: France had to get Morocco to stop work on the road that threatened

Irghiz, or else the hostage would be executed without further notice. The panicking secretary wanted to transfer me
to someone in charge, but I was out of coins.

When I returned to the house, they welcomed me like
a celebrity, a survivor. They were so afraid I'd run away.
"You believe me now? Think I was still making him up?"
the father boomed, pointing me out to the new arrivals. I
lowered my eyes modestly. And then they talked about
calling in the police, so they could take my statement. I
explained that I'd only wanted to do their son a favor, but
I'd come back to their country without legal status and
couldn't afford to be seen. They looked crushed, disappointed, even hostile.

Fortunately, the telephone rang. It was the person in
charge from Quai d'Orsay, who wanted to know if the parents of official delegate Schneider had had any news re-
cently, or a ransom demand. He said he was verifying the
authenticity of the claim, that he would find out from the
Moroccan authorities about this rebel movement, but that
for the moment they shouldn't necessarily take it seriously
or be overly concerned, and that he was doing everything
in his power.

Jean-Pierre's father hung up, tears in his eyes. His mother
rushed into his arms and he comforted her, promised her
that Jean-Pierre was being well treated and that he'd be
home soon and they'd go to Paris. She nodded against his
tears. Bitterness had been slowly killing them; hope brought
them back to life.

When the police came to the door, his mother grabbed me by the arm and rushed me upstairs to hide in her son's room. I gave her the schoolboy notebook, the travel diary. I told her that everything was in there, that it just needed to be polished up and given to a publisher. It was Jean-Pierre's wish. Now that he was a hostage, with his photo in *Paris-Match*, he had a chance of being read.

Mouth agape, she stared at the work she held in her rigid arms like a fragile infant. And then, in a shamed voice, she uttered a sentence that I didn't expect. Her lips trembling in her fleshy red face, cheeks puffed out by a smile that didn't last, she murmured, "His handwriting is too small."

I mustn't tell his father, but she couldn't read it anymore, with her poor eyesight. Would I agree to read it to her? She added that Jean-Pierre had never had a friend before me: I could stay a few days, if I had time. It would do her good to hear footsteps in the boy's room.

I had time.

At first, I thought I would simply add some footnotes to Jean-Pierre's pages, to give my view, some explanation, or an alternate version when I saw things differently. And then, at the fifteenth asterisk at the foot of the same page, when my notes ended up taking more space than his text, I decided to write a small foreword to introduce myself, in my way, as a kind of counterpoint. It seemed important to make Jean-Pierre exist in my eyes, to describe our meeting in my own words, so that people would realize.

And that's how I found myself sitting ten hours a day at his schoolboy desk, in front of the window, seeking my words in the apple tree. My story begins on page 7, to encourage me, as if I'd already written six. The plot starts off in North Marseilles. My feet too large for his slippers, fingers squeezing the pen chewed by his teeth, I narrate my life to make him a preface.

In the afternoons, his mother brings me tea with a slice of cake. She tells me the boy was crazy about it, but it isn't as good as it used to be. I protest with my mouth full. And then she adds that she doesn't mean to disturb me, and she leaves. But I can feel her eyes boring into my back, imagining him in my place, hunched spine above the old Lorfonte notebook (for as the slogan on the yellow cover goes, *"La fonte, l'or de la Lorraine"*: "Cast iron is Lorraine gold"). I pretend to write, like him, to drink his tea and love everything he loved.

One Thursday morning, Agnes came, on pretext of bringing back a casserole dish. She came up to ask me, without the others knowing, her eyes lowered, if she was in the book. The sound of her children who had broken a glass in the kitchen saved me from answering. With an exasperated sigh, before running downstairs, she said she'd come back as soon as she could.

I love the way they are all waiting, at the telephone, the mailbox, the door to my room, for news of the boy. Quai d'Orsay no longer calls, but the preface is coming along well. It's even threatening to be longer than planned.

Despite my best efforts, I can't fit Lila, the gypsies, Floral Valley, and Mr. Giraudy into three pages.

In the final account, I believe that the novel Jean-Pierre wanted to write, saying "I" in my voice, is taking shape. I even have the sense that the author is feeling more and more at home in my skin.

The days pass, unchanging. The meals are good, I have Jean-Pierre's napkin ring, and I'm starting to become familiar with the life he would have led if he'd stayed here. His father took me to visit the forge in Joeuf. It's there that they cast the cannonballs for the soldiers of Year II of the Revolution, he explained, walking across the deserted lot bristling with shrubs and littered with abandoned pig molds. When he finished telling his memories of the vanished plant where he'd started out, he blinked at the empty landscape again and grumbled, "The steel industry is what swallowed Joeuf. Just like it's going to swallow up Uckange."

And he told me an amazing story about foundries devoured by their own clients: once upon a time, the ore processed in the blast furnaces had become cast iron that supplied the ironworks; now it was the foundry itself, directly broken up into scrap metal, that they shoved into the electric furnaces to make steel. Moyeuvre, Auboué, and Harnécourt had already been melted down, and Joeuf and Uckange would be next. The century-old expertise of the best furnacemen in Europe, who used to sell their cast iron as far away as America, had turned into early retirement, layoffs, and change of profession. Young guys like Gerard were being offered a choice of two options other than steel: warehouseman in Normandy or quality control inspector at the Saupiquet fish canneries. That's what they called social betterment.

As smelting manager at Lorfonte-Uckange, Gerard preferred to restart his career as a simple mold aligner on a short-term contract in another iron foundry that had been granted a temporary reprieve.

"Can you see me inspecting the length of sardines and the number of bones in a mackerel?" he asks me. No, I can't. He's never left the Moselle, never tried to lose his accent. He looks like a taller, stockier, simpler version of Jean-Pierre. It's nice to have a brother.

On Sundays, when he comes for lunch with his wife, he teaches me to play chess. They had to be quiet when they were kids, on the many days when their father worked the night shift and recovered until sundown. To keep from making noise, Jean-Pierre wrote stories and Gerard took up chess, all by himself. He would draw lots to see if he was white or black. Sometimes he beat himself, sometimes he conceded defeat to himself. With the two of us, it was less ambiguous: he won every time.

He gets a dreamy look when he talks about Jean-Pierre. He's envied his brother since he went away. He too, if he'd had a talent that would get him out of here . . . But as the oldest, his place was to follow in his father's footsteps, in the proud tradition of the ironworks.

"You know, once you've experienced the smell of the furnace, the flow of the molten metal, the fire at your fingertips with you as its master, the sirens that run your life telling you when it's time to go join your buddies—once you've known that, you don't get used to anything else. You can't. These days, in Uckange, nobody can stand the silence. The air isn't as gray now, they tell us, since the plant isn't polluting it anymore. But the gray is in our souls."

"Put *that* in your book," his friend Guy says to me. Guy is Agnes's husband, a redhead who's been slowly killing himself with beer since he refused his social betterment: he can't go become a warehouseman in Normandy, or a surface technician in Brest, either, because of the unsalable house he's just finished paying off, Agnes's job at City Hall, the children's planned apprenticeship in his father-in-law's butcher shop . . . "Please, Aziz, write that in your book. So everyone will know."

I'm writing it.

Someday, I'll invite Agnes over to hear your last pages. She'll come into your room, sit on your bed, rediscover your voice. And she'll regret having said no to you, the day of the plaster-covered croissants. Maybe to her I'll tell the truth. I'll say that you died holding her in your arms, with her name on your lips, and that death is like that barren lot in Joeuf where ghosts still continue to cast iron.

Someday, if you like, we'll make love to her.